For information contact: info@outlawspublishing.com
Cover Art by Randy Hogue
Cover design by Outlaws Publishing.
Published by Outlaws Publishing.
September 2024
10 9 8 7 6 5 4 3 2 1

"The greatest legacy one can pass on

to one's children and grandchildren

is not money or other material things

accumulated in one's life, but

rather a legacy of character and faith"

Billy Graham

SPIRIT OF THE WOLF
A New Beginning
Volume I

RANDY HOGUE

Acknowledgements:

Thank you to my loving wife, Carole, for her support and patience in my writing.

Thank you to my independent editors and friends for the encouraging words: Marla Lee, Becky Voyles, Bethany Voyles, Evie McGovern, Chris Howard, and Thomas Hales.

And thank you to Jan Roberts for her hours of editing and tremendous help with wording and great suggestions to add into the story.

Foreword:

Alan and Odina, a young married couple set out on a journey to begin their lives in the rugged Appalachian Mountains. Follow the struggles throughout the hard times they faced, the happy times they embraced and the friendships they formed along the way.

The mysteries of the mountains and the treasures uncovered will draw you into the life of the Adams family and how they endured the hard times and dangers while raising a beautiful family without the comforts of the modern century.

The author, in this compelling story, has attempted to pay respect and homage to the journey of all people who survived the difficult times of the 18th century in the rugged Appalachian Mountains.

Some say Spirits are a means of protection, others feel Spirits are evil. What do you think?

1: A New Beginning

The day dawns as the sun peaks out over the mountains. With love, hopes and dreams, and a few dollars on hand, the journey begins for a young married couple.

Alan Atohi Adams, half Cherokee and half Scottish, was born March 11,1830 in High Point, Virginia in his family's home. Raised in High Point, he learned the ways of survival, but also attended school doing well with his education. His mother, Awinita Adams was a full-blooded Cherokee. She was fortunate not to be relocated to Oklahoma facing what was known as the Trail of Tears. Many members of her people that lived in the villages surrounding the Blue Ridge Mountain region were not as fortunate as Awinita. They were forced to relocate where many perished on the Trail of Tears.

His father, James Douglas Adams was Scottish and worked in the coal mines.

Alan learned the Cherokee language from his mother, and she taught him to show respect for the land and all wildlife. He learned from his father how to hunt, trap, track animals and people, as well as how to fish and pan for gold. At the age of eight, he went alongside his father to the coal mines. His father instilled in him the ability to survive without riches, be it money or gold.

Odina Elu Adams, a full-blooded Cherokee, was born April 15, 1832, in a tribal village in the Appalachian Mountains of Virginia. Odina and her people were allowed to remain in the Appalachian Mountains. She was raised to speak the Cherokee language of her ancestors; however, she later learned English and other subjects from a school just outside the village. At just twelve years of age, she began teaching the children in the village

English and how to read and write. The elders taught her how to cook, sew, make • jewelry and how to hunt and fish, and all the necessary survival skills.

Alan and Odina were married on March 1, 1847. Alan was seventeen, about six foot two inches tall, weighing around one hundred seventy-five pounds, lean, but muscular with an olive complexion, jet black hair and blue eyes. Odina, at fifteen years old, was of slim build, jet black hair and olive complexion and knew how to take care of herself.

Alan's parents had a little log cabin that would become their first home. Alan worked in the coal mines in High Point and utilized other skills to survive. It was a hard life, but also a life they loved.

Their dream was to have their own property, raise a family and live in harmony with the land, the people around them, and of course the wildlife. When Alan heard from his coal miner friends that a new coal mine would soon be opening in Shepherd Springs, Virginia, he was excited at the opportunity of a job. And along with the job possibility, tracts of land were available for sale, and he thought it would be a good place for them to start their new life.

The year was 1848 and they loaded their Buckboard with all their belongings, hooked up Scout and Pogo, the two horses they owned, and began their journey. Shepherd Springs was about fifty miles north of High Point, so it would take about two days to arrive. They had plans to meet with a banker in hopes of purchasing a plot of land.

Arriving in Shepherd Springs, they met Mr. Edgar Barber at the bank. He told them the parcel of land they were interested in was two hundred acres, with a small log cabin suitable for living, a nice barn for horses and livestock, a chicken coop, a smokehouse, a well near the house, and an outhouse. The property also had a freshwater spring up the hill behind the cabin that the former owner had fixed, so it would have gravity flow water to the cabin. The land, according to Mr. Barber, was full of game to hunt and trap and good fishing holes. Alan and Odina were excited and hopeful it would be something they would be able to afford. As they anxiously awaited the price, Mr. Barber explained the details. The price was one thousand two hundred seventy-five dollars, the down payment would be twenty-five dollars with a monthly payment of ten dollars a month for twelve years, however, he warned them if two payments were missed, the bank would take the land and buildings back. Since they had not seen the property, Alan asked if they could see the land before signing the contract agreement.

"I would be happy to go with you," said Mr. Barber. He wanted to help the young couple, so he would just bring the contract along and if they decided to purchase the property, they could sign the contract and make the down payment.

It was three miles out on Three Bears Trail, and Mr. Barber knew it would save them a trip back to town since they had already traveled for a long time.

Alan and Odina were excited to see the land that sounded like paradise, but were wondering why someone would leave such a place that sounded so perfect. When they arrived, it appeared to be just like Mr. Barber described it, but before they began to check out the cabin and other buildings, Alan just felt he had to ask Mr. Barber why anyone would leave this place. He told them a little bit about Fred and Edna Smith, who had owned the property. They lived there for years and over time Fred built all the things they saw. They were fine people and what happened was a tragedy. One morning, Fred left to go trapping and he was to be back in a couple of days. Of course, when he did not return, Edna began to worry, she feared the worst naturally, since she knew the terrain and they were both getting on up in years.

Mr. Barber said, "Have you met Sloppy, he and Fred were good friends, and he was the one that found Fred. He would be able to give you all the details of what happened and how Fred died. After about two years, Edna could no longer stay there, do the work and make the banknotes, so she packed up and moved to Ohio to live with her sister. The bank had no choice, but to take the property back."

As they entered the cabin, they could see all the work it took to make this a comfortable home for the Smiths and they felt sad, but then realized that this place served its purpose well for the Smiths for years and would do the same for them. Alan walked outside to explore the grounds and noted a grave on a hill outside of the cabin. As he approached the grave, the marker read, *Fred Smith, Born 1780-Died 1846.* Alan knew this was the perfect resting place for Mr. Smith and would honor it as such. With fifty dollars to their name and a few goods to trade, like the necklaces and bracelets that Odina had made they were concerned about being able to make the payments, however, they realized they could not pass this property up. Alan told Mr. Barber they were ready to sign the papers.

They sat down at the little wooden table in the cabin as Mr. Barber took out the paperwork. There was a loan sheet that described the area, the total cost and the monthly payments due after signing. He also included a plat drawing that showed the boundaries and how the corners were marked with stones stacked a couple of feet high. He explained that the deed to the property would be held at the bank until it was paid in full.

Alan paid the twenty-five-dollar deposit, signed the papers, and shook Mr. Barber's hand. He knew they had done the right thing.

It was Friday, the end of April, around noon as they watched Mr. Barber head back to Shepherd Springs. Now it was time to begin exploring his land, but first, he needed to unload the supplies they had brought along, unhook the horses from the Buckboard, take them to the barn and put them in the stable. He fed them oats and hay, and filled the trough with water he drew from the well.

Now that the chores were finished and the property purchase was completed, he began to walk around the property while it was still light, and while Odina was in the cabin cleaning and finding all kinds of items the Smiths had left behind. Alan had always liked exploring unfamiliar places and planned to do more tomorrow by horseback.

The land was approximately two hundred acres of hill country in the middle of the Appalachian Mountain region and about two miles from the Potomac River. There was a small section of the land that was flat enough to plant crops on, but they would need a mule to plow the ground.

In two more days, it would be time to meet with Joseph Stockburn, the President of the new coal mining company in Shepherd Springs about a job at the new mine that would be opening soon. The new mine was just a mile out of Shepherd Springs. With the salary he would earn, he could better provide for the family they hoped to have soon. His skill in hunting, fishing, and trapping would help to provide, also, and Odina hoped to sell the beautiful jewelry she made to strangers passing through town.

2. The Town of Shepherd Springs

The population of Shepherd Springs in 1848 was about sixty people with most living on the outskirts of town. There was a General Merchandise Store owned by Liam Dobbs; a Trading Post owned by Jack Bennings, who everyone called Beanstalk because of his height. Wilbur Williams ran the Post Office and was also the Telegraph Operator, in the same building. The Doctor's office and drug store was where Doctor Lovie Hogue tended to patients. Dr. Hogue lived above the drug store in an apartment. Franklin Cooper was the druggist in Shepherd Springs. There was a six-room hotel with a dining room owned and operated by Nathan and Cora-Mae Tibbs. Visitors that passed through town could bed down and have a meal. It was also frequently visited by the town folks. The marshal's office was on the right side of the hotel and Neil McCall was the town marshal. On the left side of the hotel was the Shepherd Springs Bank. Edgar Barber was the bank President, and his assistant teller was Theodore Baker. Moving on to the north end of town was the Primitive Baptist Church where Preacher John Woods delivered the Sunday sermons. A little single room schoolhouse across from the church was where Ms. Ella Styles taught all the children how to read and write. On the south end was the Livery Stables and the Blacksmith Shop operated by Jacob Jenkins. Then, there was the Carpenter's Shop where Delmar Betts made furniture and built coffins when needed. The last shop next to Delmar's was a small tavern called Roosters Tavern owned and operated by Rooster Firewater Jones.

After learning all about the town, he again began exploring his land, but dark was approaching and it was time to stop and check the barn, the chicken coop, the smokehouse and the back of the cabin for any tools that may have been left behind to give him a better idea of what he would need later once they were more settled in. There were two wooden buckets, a pitchfork, one hoe, a shovel, an ax and over in the corner of the barn he noticed two pans that he knew were used to pan for gold. Alan was a bit confused since this area was not known for gold mining unless Ol' Mr. Smith knew something that he never told anyone about. Prospectors were always known to be secretive about any gold they found and the location where it was found.

He knew he must get the strike rich notion out of his head about finding gold on his place, for now, he had a lot to do to get settled in before meeting with Mr. Stockburn on Monday about the job.

Walking over to the smokehouse and chicken coop, he noticed both were empty, but there was a lingering smell of hickory, probably from the Smiths using it to cure and smoke meat. Next on the list would be getting laying hens for eggs. Heading back to the cabin he noticed smoke coming out of a stove pipe on the back side of the cabin. A bit curious, he began trying to recall everything he saw when they first entered the cabin with Mr. Barber. There was a rock fireplace located at the right end, plus there was the wooden table with two chairs in the middle of the room against the back wall that he and Mr. Barber used to complete the paperwork on the purchase. All the way over to the left was a rope bed with a mattress packed full of cotton and over the head of the bed was a loft with a ladder for steps to the loft. Alan was, at that time, more interested on the outside and never looked in the back room that was added on years ago, but Odina did. The size of the cabin was about sixteen feet wide and twenty-four feet long and the back room that was added was eight feet wide and twenty-four feet long. The loft would serve well as sleeping quarters for the children they both wanted and plan to have in the future.

3. First Meal in the New Home

Alan entered the back door of the cabin and noticed a light coming from inside and immediately smelled Odina's cooking. His beautiful wife was standing over the wood burning stove smiling. She looked and asked if he was hungry. Alan stood there in silence smiling, admiring his wife and thinking how lucky he was. Odina had found an iron skillet, two coal oil lamps, some wood for the stove and other cooking utensils. She had taken two slices of bacon off a slab of cured bacon, fried it in the iron skillet, made flat bread and roasted two ears of corn. As they sat down at the old wooden table for supper, they began talking about the supplies they would be needing soon to survive and remembering that twenty-five dollars was all they had left. They needed to put ten dollars up for the next month's bank payment, so they actually only had fifteen dollars to use for the next month.

After supper, they sat on the front porch admiring the stars that seemed closer and listening to the sounds of the night in the Appalachian Mountains and knew this was their paradise. There was a chill in the air as they turned in for the night, but the blankets would keep them warm. The rope bed with the cotton stuffed mattress felt like they were laying on a soft fluffy cloud. Alan and Odina were tired from traveling, but excited for their new life and home as they fell asleep happy and content. Waking up at daybreak to the sounds of the mountains that surrounded them, they felt refreshed and ready to start the day. Odina started a fire in the wood burning stove and the warmth of the stove felt good as she prepared breakfast of bacon and flat bread. She also brought along some sassafras leaves and roots to make sassafras tea. Alan liked his coffee in the mornings, but until they were able to buy coffee, the tea would have to do for now.

After breakfast, it was time to head out to the barn to check on the horses. Behind the barn there was a large section that was fenced with plenty of green grass for grazing but first he needed to check out the fence line before releasing the horses into the area. Walking along the fence line, he noticed a pool of water in the far corner of the pasture. He assumed Mr. Smith had dug out a hole so he could reach the spring and once he was able to do that, it would be enough to provide water for the livestock. He continued to walk the entire fence line making sure there were no open places the horses could get through. After he was satisfied the fence was secure, he went back to the barn and released both horses into the pasture.

Alan headed back to the cabin and once again, he smelled the bacon cooking.

Entering through the back door, he could see the happiness on Odina's face, and he knew she was just as happy as he was to be here.

4. Fishing Hole and Property lines

After breakfast, Alan went to the front porch to sit and sip on his cup of tea. He could see Three Bears Trail from his front porch but, so far, he had not noticed anyone riding by. There was a redtail hawk high above the hilltop and he watched as it dove down to the ground and grabbed a rabbit. Thinking to himself that will be the hawk's breakfast.

There was still a lot to do to get prepared for the days to come but he really wanted to explore the rest of the land. He remembered Mr. Barber saying there was a good-sized creek on the property for fishing. Well, it was time to stop daydreaming, and head back to the barn, and call Scout, knowing he could make better time on horseback if he could find trails on the steep mountains to travel on. Scout and Pogo both came when he called but, on this adventure, he would only need Scout. He made a couple of fish hooks out of some stiff wire he had, plus added several feet of small strong string and he was ready to go. For protection he always carried his handmade knife with an eight-inch blade and deer antlers for handles in a sheath on his belt along with his model 1848 Colt Revolver 44 caliber.

With the plat drawing of his land in his pocket, he headed northwest to find the lower corner marker. He located the marker by seeing rocks stacked up about two feet tall just as Mr. Barber described, then he headed due north. Traveling to the northwest corner was easy for Scout, but going northeast was different. The hills were steep, and they were forced to go around some and sideways on others. As he topped the ridge, he heard the crashing sound of a waterfall and found it easily, he was excited to see that the waterfall was on his property. As he got closer, he could see what he thought would be about a forty-foot waterfall coming off the steep mountain side. At the bottom was a deep hole of water and it continued to flow down the mountain valley as a swift running creek. He was pretty sure the creek ran into the Potomac River about two miles away, but he would need to check that out on another day since he wanted to fish today in the deep hole. Alan cut a sapling that was about eight feet long, then tied six feet of line to the end and attached his homemade hook. Next, he needed bait, so he rolled over a rotten log and found a couple of grub worms. As he slid down the bank to reach a sandbar, he noticed fresh bear tracks. The bear tracks were large, and he thought he may have scared the bear off when he came over the hill. He was glad to know he had a bear on his land as long as the bear did not damage his home searching for food. Alan was finally ready to begin fishing, he baited his hook with a grub worm and flung it out as far as the eight-foot sapling would let him. He watched the grub worm slowly sink down then suddenly; he felt a fish hit. He pulled a two-pound rainbow trout out of the hole on the first cast. He removed the trout and baited up again watching the grub worm slowly sink and bam, another fish hit. When he pulled it out of the hole, it looked to be about another two-pound trout. This would be plenty for supper tonight, so he stopped, took his fishing pole and leaned it against a tree at the fishing hole. His goal now was to find the northern corner marker before he headed back to the cabin.

Looking at the plat drawing again, Alan could tell he needed to cross the creek and continue north, then try to go east toward the top of the steep mountain. He hopped on Scout, crossed the creek and headed north until he felt he was at his property line then he would go east. Having the plat drawing had made it easy to find the markers. Going up the side of the mountain to the top was hard traveling for Scout but once they reached the top, Alan found his north marker of two feet high stacked rocks. Now, all he must find is the southeast corner marker so he would know all his land. He hopped back on Scout and headed south down the ridge that would take him to the mountain tops behind his cabin and from there he could go on to the southeast corner marker. As he was slowly riding down the ridge, he couldn't help but think about those two pans for gold mining he found and wondered if Ole Mr. Smith had found gold on the land, but he didn't have enough time now to start chasing that dream. Riding on Scout was a lot quicker than walking but walking all his land would come many times in the future. He knew he was getting close to the southeast corner as he began going down the ridge to cross a holler, then he started up another ridge that wasn't as steep. After about one hundred yards, he could see four white tail deer running down the mountain.

The deer were bedded down at the top of the ridge, but took off when they heard Alan and Scout coming their way. Everything Alan had seen on their place made him more and more sure that this was indeed a paradise, and he knew he would be able to provide plenty of food for his family.

A short distance in front of him he spotted the rocks that were stacked two feet tall which he knew was for the southeast corner marker. Alan had now located all four corners of his property but still had not seen all the land yet. He headed down the mountain to the west which he thought should be close to his southern boundary line and there he ran into Three Bears Trail. Turning to his right on Three Bears Trail, he could see where his property line was. In a few minutes' time, he would be able to see his cabin up on the rise and the path that would take him there. He decided to go past the path to his cabin to check out the section of bottom land where he planned to plant his crops. When he reached the section, it was about three acres. Alan could tell that Mr. Smith planted a lot of crops there since all the big rocks had been removed from the piece of ground and stacked on the western border to form a rock wall about two feet tall and three hundred feet long. The soil appeared to be very fertile, and he was thinking he would plant corn and potatoes but, that probably would not happen in time to plant this year since he still did not have a mule.

5. Treasures in Paradise

Alan hopped back on Scout and rode up to the back of the Cabin where he let Scout get a drink of water from the trough behind the cabin and he took a drink using the dipper that was hanging close by.

Odina stepped out the back door and saw the trout he had brought home. She was thrilled at the sight and said, "We will have a great supper." As Alan approached her, he could tell she had this excited look on her face as if there was something she wanted to tell him. It seemed Odina had done some exploring herself while he was gone. She had walked to the back and base of the mountain behind their cabin and found a lot of blackberry bushes. Also, on the mountain side, she found huckleberry bushes, which would be good when they ripened. Alan was happy about the good things that kept happening, but Odina was still smiling and giggling a little as if there was something more to tell.

Alan finally said to Odina, "What else are you smiling about my love? Did you find an apple tree or a pear tree on your adventure?"

Odina said, "No," she came back to the cabin to do more cleaning and organizing and while she was straightening out around the rock fireplace, she moved the wooden firewood box to clean underneath and make sure no creatures were hiding there when she noticed the floor plank was loose; not nailed down. She then lifted the plank and saw a small wooden box in the hole under the plank. There were two cloth tobacco pouches inside. Odina handed the two cloth tobacco pouches to Alan and asked him what he thought they were, but she already knew the answer. As he opened the pouches, his eyes got really big, and he knew then that Mr. Smith had found gold somewhere on the property or close by.

They had no idea what the value of the gold in the pouches was or how to go about selling or exactly where they could sell it, but they also knew they had to be careful and not talk about it to anyone right now. They first would need to meet and get to know the people in town, pay attention and listen and hopefully they could find someone they could trust. Alan was thinking of riding into Shepherd Springs after he returned from his adventure of the land to pick up some more supplies, they would need soon but decided against it since they only had fifteen dollars left to live on for the next month.

Their food supply left consisted of about four pounds of cornmeal, four pounds of flour, ten pounds of potatoes, eight roasting ears of corn, ten pounds of cured slab of bacon, and a bag of dried sassafras leaves and roots for tea. They also brought other items with them such as, bed linens, wool blankets, a couple of quilts, cooking utensils, tin plates and cups, a coffee pot, clothing, sewing supplies, a fifty caliber Hawkins Rifle, a Colt forty-four caliber Revolver, a homemade knife with an eight-inch blade and about thirty pounds of grain and oats for the horses. They felt very fortunate that so many needed items were left at the cabin, and they still were finding more useful and needed things.

They both should be tired by now, but they were young, excited and still full of energy. Odina began to prepare the fish for supper along with potatoes cooked in bacon grease and flat bread. They would have cool spring water with supper, instead of sassafras tea, as it had a tendency to energize them too much and might interfere with sleep. Since it would be a while before supper, Alan decided he needed to cut more stove wood, their stack was getting low, and they had to have it for cooking. He went outside and cut enough to last for a few days. Then he took Scout back to the pasture to graze and decided to look at everything in the barn plus the lean sheds on each side of the barn when he realized he never noticed there was another wagon on the right side of the barn at the back of the lean to. The wagon was a little bigger than his Buckboard and looked to be in good shape. It was loaded down with planks of wood that he could surely use to build anything needed. Hanging on the outside of the barn under the lean to he found two crosscut saws, one was a two man saw and the other was for only one man. Alan had noticed a stand for holding logs behind the cabin, he knew he could definitely use the saws there. Cutting wood with a cross saw was just as tiring as cutting it with an ax but it was faster and easier to cut the short lengths, they needed for the wood stove. He climbed up to the loft and saw a pile of hay there. In the back corner, he noticed four wooden chairs in good shape, a couple of small wooden boxes and he got excited thinking about what Odina had found in the box hidden in the cabin. As he opened the first box, he saw it had some very pretty stones of red, green and turquoise and he couldn't wait to show Odina the stones he had found, another treasure. He felt sure she could use them to make jewelry. The next box he opened had two pieces of folded paper inside.

The first paper he unfolded had a drawing of what appeared to be of his land, it looked the same as the plat drawing with an X marked on it. The second paper he unfolded was the same drawing, but it had an X marked in a different spot. Now, Alan was excited. It could mean absolutely nothing, or it could be something special. He climbed down from the loft taking the two wooden boxes with him as he walked back up to the cabin. When he reached the cabin, he placed the two boxes on the front porch and went inside. Odina heard him come in and told him supper was ready. He didn't want to tell her about his findings yet, he decided to wait until they finished supper and were sitting on the porch, then he would show her the boxes. They sat down at the little wooden table and enjoyed a meal that was delicious and filling. After they were finished, Odina began to clean the tin plates and bowls when Alan asked her to do the clean up later and come sit on the porch with him for a few minutes and listen to the sounds of the Appalachians. She really wanted to finish her work first, but he convinced her to come and sit for a few minutes. Odina could see the excitement on his face as he handed her the first box with the pretty stones inside. When she opened it and saw all the stones, her eyes lit up and the biggest smile came across her face, she was excited too. It was hard to see the beautiful colors since it was already dark on the porch. They went inside where the coal oil lamp was burning to get a better look. Alan told Odina they would become more beautiful in the sunlight. He then opened the other box that held the two papers folded and explained to her the X mark on each paper might just be the place where the stones and maybe the gold was found. Alan pulled out the original drawing of the plat of their land and it was the same shape so he knew he could find the X locations with a little exploring. They decided to put the papers in the box with the stones and place them in the same hiding place as the box with the gold in it.

6. Pay Attention to the Sounds

Odina began to finish cleaning all the cooking utensils as Alan headed back to the front porch. It was a full moon, and he could see the cross marker on Fred Smith's grave up on the hill beside their cabin, he decided to walk up the hill to the grave. He wasn't sure why he was there, but he hoped he could maybe communicate with Fred Smith's spirit and get answers to what all the goodness meant. The wind began blowing and Alan could hear the leaves rustling in the trees when he heard what sounded like a Wolf howling from deep in the forest of the mountains. The howling sound of the Wolf came from near where the waterfall area was. Alan knew that the Red Wolf used to live in the mountain region, but he believed they had been eradicated fifty years ago. He had never seen any tracks on his place or even in High Point, Virginia where he grew up. He remembered as a young boy hearing the elders talk of the spirit of the Wolf before they became extinct from the region. As he began to walk back down the hill to the cabin, he paused at the porch, something was telling him to look back up to Fred Smith's grave and since there was a full moon, he could clearly see the cross marker at Fred's grave. A misty fog was lying over the hill and the grave when he saw a figure of a large Wolf standing over Fred's grave as if it was Fred's protector. Alan could not believe what he had just seen but just as quickly as it appeared, it was gone. He respected the Spirit of the Wolf; he had no fear of it.

Alan entered the front door of the cabin and was getting ready for bed but was thinking of all the happiness of the last two amazing days and was still smiling. With the light of the full moon shining through the windows of the cabin he could see his beautiful wife lying on the bed waiting for him. He knew his amazement had not yet ended.

It was breaking day on Sunday morning May 2, 1848, and it was cold in the cabin. Alan was first out of bed and started a fire in the wood stove to warm the cabin while Odina was starting breakfast. Alan poured a cup of spring water and went out onto the front porch to breathe in the fresh mountain air when, off in the distance, he heard the howl of the Wolf again coming from the same area.

This time he was certain it was not his imagination. He could feel there was something special about the Spirit of the Wolf.

Odina had finished frying up a few slices of bacon and more flat bread and called Alan to breakfast. The bacon and bread would fill their hunger and the sassafras tea she made would boost their energy.

7. First Friend

After breakfast, Alan poured another warm cup of sassafras tea and stepped out onto the front porch while Odina cleaned up the breakfast dishes. The front porch seemed to be where he could get his best thinking done. As he looked down across the valley, Alan spotted a man on horseback pulling a pack mule behind him coming down Three Bears Trail. This was the first person he had seen since arriving here except for Mr. Barber from the bank. He watched as he turned and started up the path to his cabin. He could see the man looked to be maybe in his fifties and was wearing buckskin britches with fringe on each side, and a buckskin shirt with fringes down the sleeves. He had a floppy hat on and a leather belt around his waist. There was a knife in a sheath on one side and a revolver on the other side. Alan could see a muzzle loading rifle in a scabbard attached to his saddle. As mean as he looked, Alan somehow knew he meant no harm to him or Odina. When he got closer to the front porch, he stopped his horse and said, "Howdy," to which Alan replied, "Howdy." The old man asked if he was any kin to Fred and Edna.

Alan told him he wasn't, that he and his wife bought the place from the bank. He was anxious to talk with this old man since he knew Fred and Edna Smith and just maybe he could learn more from him.

They exchanged greetings with Alan telling him his name was Alan Adams and his wife was Odina.

The old man said he was Willard Floyd, but everybody just called him Sloppy, and he said, "I'm pleased to meet you young man."

Alan told Sloppy how good it was to meet him and offered him a cup of sassafras tea and to sit on the porch with him and rest a bit. He would offer him coffee, but they didn't have any, so it was tea in the mornings for now.

Ole Sloppy hopped off his horse, thanked Alan, and said, "A cup of tea would be good." Before walking up to the porch, he went back to his mule and untied a burlap bag and handed it to Alan. He said, "Tell your Misses to scoop out a big cup or two of coffee so you can have some for later."

Alan thanked him for the coffee and thought about the plans he had for the day, but he felt like talking with Sloppy was more important. He asked Sloppy what type of work he did, and he told him he was a trapper and sold his pelts in town at the Trading Post. He also did a little prospecting when he could, even though gold was hard to find in this area, but he had found some beautiful gemstones.

Sloppy went on to tell Alan about going to Shepherd Springs yesterday with his pelts he had trapped a few months ago and trading them for food, supplies, coffee, ammunition, chewing tobacco and a little money. He had worked in the coal mines and sawmills when he was younger but for the last thirty years, he had been living off the land in the Appalachian Mountains.

When Alan asked where he lived, he pointed North to the mountains indicating that was his home. Sloppy noticed the confused look on Alan's face, he laughed and said, "I have a little cabin, but nobody knows about it or where it is, and I have never seen any humans anywhere close to it."

Alan was worried he was sounding too nosey asking all the questions to a stranger, but he asked if he knew how Fred died.

Sloppy said it was normal for Fred to go off trapping for a few days, then check back in with Edna before heading out again. This time he told Edna he would only be gone for a couple of days because the trap line he was going to was just a little past his north boundary line and he would be camping in the woods. Then Sloppy began to tell Alan the story of finding Fred. He was heading to town one day and stopped at Fred's place to see his old friend when Edna told him Fred had been gone for six days and she was worried since he was only supposed to be gone for a couple of days. They both knew that Fred could take care of himself and survive in the mountains, but they also knew he meant what he said and if he's four days late something had probably happened to him. Sloppy knew that too because the mountains could be unforgiving with hidden dangers. He told Edna he would head out to the north and try to find him. Sloppy said he rode his horse as far as he could and found Fred's camp, some of his traps and tools but it did not appear that he had been there for a few days. He told Alan he yelled out for Fred and when he didn't get a reply, he began walking north. As he started walking north again, he went up the first mountain about halfway then on to the side looking for a sign of where Fred may have put his traps out for the foxes and bobcats, and he yelled out for him every few hundred yards. As he was standing, quiet and listening, he heard the very distinct sound of a Wolf howling just up the ridge from where he was standing. Sloppy went on to say he had never seen a wolf track or a wolf in this area and he had been in the mountains for almost thirty years, but he was familiar with the sound. He went on about three hundred yards closer to the sound of the howling Wolf and found Fred pinned under a fallen tree. He had been dead for a few days.

Sloppy said, "Of all the things in the wild that could harm you, what are the odds of a tree falling on you?" He spoke of standing over his friend in silence and giving thanks to the Spirit of the Wolf for leading him to Fred. At the location of Fred's body, he began to dig a trench next to it; then he dug under his body until he could drag his friend out from under the tree. He built a drag sled, or as the Indians called it, a travois by cutting two saplings about twelve to fourteen foot long then he placed several braces across from pole to pole. Once he secured the drag sled to his horse and loaded his friend on the sled, he again secured him with the rope he had left. Then he started the slow ride back to Fred's home.

As he approached Fred's cabin, he could see Edna on the porch and the town marshal, Neil McCall, standing with a couple of volunteers that were ready to search for Fred.

Edna screamed out, "Oh No!" and began weeping.

He explained to them how Fred died and said he was so sorry because he was a good friend.

Marshal McCall told Edna he could take Fred's body to Dr. Hogue so he could write the death certificate and have the undertaker prepare him for burial.

Sloppy said Edna was very thankful to Marshal McCall for taking care of that part for her, but she wanted his body brought back to be buried on the hill beside the cabin. Edna then hugged him and thanked him for finding Fred and bringing him home. "Now that's the best I remember," said Sloppy.

Alan could tell Ole Sloppy was feeling bad reliving the death of his friend, so he didn't want to ask him anymore, even though he had a lot of questions that only Sloppy could probably answer. He drank down the last of the sassafras tea and said, "tell the Misses thanks for the tea, it was mighty good, but I better be on my way now."

Alan told him how good it was to meet him and to stop by anytime he was back this way, he really enjoyed talking with him. He, also, told him he was going into town tomorrow morning to meet with Mr. Stockburn about a job at the new coal mine, but today he wanted to go back to a fishing hole at the northwest end of the property and try to catch a few trout for supper.

Sloppy smiled, he knew where the fishing hole was and told him about the beautiful waterfall that dumps water into the fishing hole and about a half mile further to the northwest he would see Fred's old camp, Fred built it well so it should still be standing. As Sloppy was walking to his horse, Alan had to ask one more thing. "How come folks call you Sloppy?"

He smiled as he turned to answer and said, "I don't rightly know, but maybe it is because I dress so nicely and have tobacco stains on the front of my shirt." And just like that, he hopped on his horse and rode off, pulling his mule behind. Alan laughed at his wit and knew he had made a friend. He was so pleased he had met an old friend of Fred Smith and wanted to know much more about him. What really got his attention was when Sloppy spoke of hearing the howling of the Wolf and how it helped him find his friend. He was confident now that the Spirit of the Wolf did exist in the Appalachian Mountains. He also could tell those two friends trusted each other till the end.

8. Alan and Odina-Fishing & Exploring

It was Sunday, May the 2nd mid-morning and Alan decided he wanted to go to the fishing hole again and catch more fish. He asked Odina to come along with him, he wanted to show her the beautiful waterfall and that part of their land.

Odina was thrilled; she loved exploring and fishing just as much as he did. She went to the kitchen to put a couple pieces of leftover bacon and flatbread in a cloth bag to take with them while Alan went to the barn to saddle up Scout. Odina always preferred to ride Pogo bareback. He loaded Scout's saddle bags with a few more homemade hooks and extra lines. He also added the two gold pans just in case they wanted to try panning for gold. They were loaded up and off to see the beautiful waterfall and fishing hole. It didn't take long by horseback; and as they rode over a small hill, they could hear the water falling off the mountain.

Alan knew they had reached a special place and turned to see Odina's face. She was all smiles with her eyes opened wide and amazed at such a beautiful place. He loved seeing his wife so happy and continued to be in awe of the beauty that surrounded them everywhere and how lucky they were to be here. They rode on over fifty more yards and arrived at the fishing hole. Alan found the fishing pole he left there, he just needed to make another one. As he was making the fishing pole, Odina was raking through the leaves and turning over old rotten logs and spotted some beetles. She grabbed one, baited her hook and slid down the bank to get on the large sandbar beside the fishing hole when she noticed the bear tracks that Alan had seen the day before. She threw her line out as far as she could and saw the beetle was floating and moving its legs, suddenly, splash, a fish bites. She pulled in a sunfish as large as her hand and told Alan it would be good eating, to bring more bait. He raked through the leaves and rotten logs to find two more beetles and a grub worm and slid down the bank to fish with her. Within a few minutes they caught two more sunfish and a rainbow trout which was about a pound. They decided they had enough, so it was time to stop.

Alan wanted to continue north and try to find Fred's camp site that Sloppy told him about. Odina wanted to stay and explore some more. She told him to just leave her one of the gold pans and the Colt Revolver in case the bear came back and if she got bored, she would follow his tracks to where he was.

He left and started out to find Fred's camp carrying his Hawkins Rifle just in case it was needed. He figured Fred's camp should be just a half a mile from the fishing hole according to Sloppy so it shouldn't take him long to find it. Within about fifteen minutes he rode up on what he knew had to be Fred's old camp. He could see a stream of crystal-clear water running through it next to the hut he had built to sleep in. He also found several steel traps hanging on a tree. At the front of the hut was an ax and a shovel, more rope and a small roll of steel wire. He thought Sloppy must have put the ax and shovel back when he came through with Fred's body. He could, also, see the fire pit between the hut and the stream. Fred's hut was built like a lean-to and was still intact. He looked inside and found a couple of wool blankets folded up in the corner and under the blankets he found another gold pan. He knew this camp was not on his land, but he felt like he was onto something that Fred knew and nobody else did. He assumed the government owned the land since not many folks could or would live in this area except for a mountain man. Alan walked downstream a little further to investigate more before heading back to Odina. In looking around, it appeared to be a good hunting and trapping area and just maybe a good place to pan for gold. He headed back to Odina, leaving behind all the items he found at Fred's camp.

Arriving back at the fishing hole he could see Odina with a lot of vines rolled up like a rope and he knew exactly what she planned to do with those. Alan asked what she had found, and Odina told him she went downstream a few hundred yards and found the wild wisteria vines she could use to make baskets they could sell or trade. They loaded up all the vines and the fish they had caught, left their fishing poles there, and started back home nibbling on the flatbread and bacon as they rode. They were so excited, they forgot to eat at the fishing hole.

Arriving home, Odina put the vines on the front porch and took the fish to the kitchen to cook while Alan put the horses in the pasture. He knew they would need more wood in a couple of days, so he grabbed the one man crosscut saw off the wall at the barn, took a couple large limbs that were on the ground behind the cabin, placed them on the stand and sawed the limbs in short pieces for the stove. As he was sawing the wood, his mind was thinking about getting some laying hens for eggs, a milk cow or maybe some goats for milk. He also needed a mule for plowing and maybe a few pigs for slaughter, but that would take more money than the fifteen dollars they had.

That brought him to think about the two small tobacco bags of gold and the one full bag of different colored gemstones. He wondered what the value of those could be and was hoping to get an idea when he met his new friend Sloppy, but was afraid to ask too much too soon until he knew he could gain his trust.

The meeting with Mr. Stockburn was tomorrow morning at about eight. After his meeting, he planned on walking around town, hoping he could meet some of the town people and maybe find out who he could sell gold and gemstones to and get an idea of how much money it would bring without talking too much. Alan knew he would not sleep tonight; his brain would be thinking of all the things he hoped to learn tomorrow.

Odina prepared fish, corn fritters and potatoes and called Alan to supper.

He came in and brought an armload of stove wood and put it into the wood box beside the little wooden tables and sat down to enjoy the meal with his amazing wife.

After they finished eating, he kissed Odina's cheek, told her how good the meal was, and headed to the front porch to admire the view of the evening while wondering how tomorrow would go.

In a few minutes, Odina joined him on the porch, put her arms around him and told him it was time for bed, he needed to get an early start in the morning. He was happy to comply with her orders and despite all he was thinking about, fell right to sleep.

9. The Job Interview

Alan was up before daylight and started a fire in the wood stove. Odina was up a few minutes later starting breakfast and she made a pot of coffee with the coffee Sloppy gave them. He told Odina he only wanted coffee, no breakfast, but asked if she wanted to ride into town with him.

Odina declined, she wanted to begin making baskets out of the vines she collected the day before.

He headed to the front porch with his coffee savoring the aroma and taste as he watched daylight appear. He could see Three Bears Trail and beyond to the beautiful valley of the Appalachians. When he focused his eyes back to Three Bears Trail, he spotted three bears going northwest on the trail. Alan laughed and thought to himself it must be how the trail got its name.

It looked to be a sow with two cubs, and he knew it wasn't the same bear that left its tracks on the sandbar at the fishing hole 'cause those tracks were much bigger, probably an old boar or maybe a daddy bear to the cubs.

He didn't have a pocket watch for telling time, but he had plans to meet Mr. Stockburn around eight o'clock at the Tibbs Hotel and Dining Hall in Shepherd Springs, so he must be on his way soon, maybe a little early, but it's always better than being late. Being truthful and honest had always been his way. Alan was also thinking he should carry a small amount of the gold with him to see if there was a buyer in town, but he would not be quite as truthful, he would not mention where the gold came from. He sure didn't want to cause a gold rush to his property so if anyone asked, it was a wedding gift from his parents in High Point, Virginia; he didn't want to lie, but prospectors are secretive for their own protection. Alan retrieved one of the tobacco pouches and emptied half the gold into another pouch and placed it in his pocket. He went to the barn and saddled up Scout for the three-mile ride into town and let Odina know he was leaving the Hawkins Rifle propped up inside the door in case she needed it. She handed him a cloth bag filled with flat bread and a couple slices of bacon to carry with him, gave him a kiss and sent him on his way.

After riding about two miles southeast on the trail, he noticed what would be his closest neighbor's homestead on the right. He hoped to have time soon to meet them. Another mile and he arrived in Shepherd Springs.

After tying Scout to a hitching post in front of the hotel, he walked into the dining hall where a few people were having breakfast when he noticed one gentleman sitting by himself at a table. They made eye contact, and the gentleman asked if he was Adams. "Yes," he said, "I am Alan Adams from High Point, I am living here now and asked if he was Mr. Stockburn."

He said, "Yes," he was indeed Joseph Stockburn and invited Alan to sit down and talk. Mr. Stockburn asked if he would like breakfast, but Alan politely said no, he didn't have money, he had some flat bread and bacon in his saddle bag for later. As Cora Mae Tibbs came to take their order, Mr. Stockburn ordered two breakfast plates of scrambled eggs, country ham, biscuits, and gravy along with two coffees. Alan was just about to speak up when Mr. Stockburn told Ms. Tibbs to put it all on his tab. He told Alan that he was highly recommended from experienced miners in High Point and asked how old he was.

He said, "I'm eighteen years old Sir."

"Well, you are such a young man," said Mr. Stockburn, "tell me about your coal mining experience?"

Alan told him he started working in the coal mines alongside his father when he was eight years old and was pretty much on his own by the time he reached twelve. He went to school in town every day to learn how to read, write, add, subtract, multiply and divide, then, he went to the coal mines to work after school. He had his own crew to supervise and make sure all safety measures were followed by the time he was sixteen. When the mines closed, off and on, he would use that time to hunt, fish, trap and help farm on his father's land. He was only paid when the mines were up and running so when they closed, he did other things to make money.

Mr. Stockburn liked what he heard, and it was exactly what his old coal miner' friends had told him about Alan when they recommended him for the job. He had purchased the mining rights of roughly one thousand acres of mountainous land one mile north of town and close to the railroad, so they could haul coal to the railroad for shipping to buyers all over the southeast. He said according to his crews that inspected the land for coal, they believe some of the mountains are solid coal and just covered with a little dirt and trees. The surveyors told him there should be ten to fifteen years of work ahead and they had already started hauling lumber to where the start of the mine would be. They would begin to build storage buildings for tools, a mining office and a separate building for storing dynamite. Mr. Stockburn offered Alan the job if he wanted it, the pay would be two dollars and fifty cents a week, a total of ten dollars a month.

Alan was excited and assured him he wanted the job, which was the reason he moved to Shepherd Springs and bought his plot of land three miles from there.

He added Alan's name to the others on the paper and asked if he knew anything about the building business, they had several buildings going up.

Alan said, "I do, I'm not one to brag, but there isn't much I can't do when I set my mind to it, I have helped build houses, barns, sheds and almost anything that was needed at the time."

Mr. Stockburn was pleased, he could start work next week helping with the buildings and the little shanties that some of the miners would need for living quarters. The actual mining work would start in about a month, but his pay would start next week. Alan inquired as to where the new mining site was located, he needed to know where to report to the next Monday. Mr. Stockburn gave him directions, and by looking at them, he knew the site would be easy to find. Alan finished up the fine breakfast while feeling guilty that Odina was not there to enjoy it with him, but he got up from the table, shook Mr. Stockburn's hand, thanked him for the breakfast and the job.

Mr. Stockburn said, "You're very welcome and I'll see you soon."

10. The Trading Post

After leaving the hotel, he realized it would be a little longer than he originally thought before he would get the first payday, so he had to figure out the best way to feed them until then. He began walking to where Scout was tied, he mounted up and since it was still early, he decided to ride north to find the new mining site. He located it about fifteen minutes later and saw stacks of sawmill lumber stacked up in different piles. Leaving the site, he headed back to town, he wanted to go to the Trading Post where his new friend Sloppy always traded and sold pelts.

The Trading Post was right next to the General Store, and he walked in. Inside he could see fur pelts hanging on the wall, a glass showcase with a few Colt Revolvers, knives, jewelry that wasn't as nice as Odina's and tools of all kinds hanging on the walls. There was so much stuff it was hard to see it all, he continued looking around and noticed a set of scales on the wooden counter that might be used for weighing gold plus there was a big safe on the floor behind the counter and he wondered if it could be full of gold.

A tall middle aged man came out from a back room of the building and said, "Hey neighbor."

Alan said, "Hello friend," He explained he was new in town, he and his wife had just bought a place three miles out on Three Bears Trail and he came to town this morning to meet with Mr. Stockburn about a job at the new coal mine and wanted to meet folks in town.

"Well son, "I am Jack Bennings, but most people call me Beanstalk, I guess because I'm so tall." He welcomed him to Shepherd Springs where almost everybody was friendly and told him he had owned and done business at the Trading Post for years.

Beanstalk said, "You said your place was three miles out on Three Bears Trail, you must have bought Fred and Edna's place."

Alan said, "Yes sir, that's my place."

Beanstalk went on to tell him about Fred, he was a good man and a good friend, and they did a lot of trading together for years.

Alan asked him what most people sold or traded to him, and Beanstalk said he traded or bought about anything he could make money on. When travelers come through town they most always came to his place and would purchase something, especially the Indian jewelry. He didn't get much gold or gemstones in, but if he did, he bought or traded for it, he had a buyer up north that would buy every ounce he could get and another company that would buy all the pelts he could get.

Alan wanted to know more about what gold would normally bring.

Beanstalk said he paid eighteen dollars an ounce for gold, but it was rare to get much gold in this area, it wasn't known for any big veins, prospectors might dig and pan for a year and still not get but a few ounces.

Alan explained he and his father had done prospecting in High Point and knew that was right; it took a long time and a lot of work to get a few ounces. He knew his food supply was getting low and no money would be coming in for a while, so he pulled out the tobacco bag from his pocket and asked Beanstalk what it would bring.

His eyes got big, he smiled and said, "Well let's weigh it and then I can tell you."

Alan said go ahead, he needed some food supplies and would like to find some laying hens and a milk cow pretty soon but he wouldn't be getting a payday for a month.

Beanstalk poured the gold out on the scale and smiled when he could see it was more flakes than dust. He looked at the scale, it was just a little over four ounces, did some figuring on paper and came up with seventy-four dollars.

Alan said he would take it.

Beanstalk carefully brushed the gold off the scales into another small cloth bag using a funnel, then opened the safe and pulled out seventy-four dollars.

That was the most money Alan had ever had, he looked around the Trading Post some more just to see if there was anything else they could use in the cabin. He asked about candles he could use for lighting in their cabin.

Beanstalk pulled out a box of candles, they were three for a dime or for twenty-five cents he could have all seven candles and two packs of long stick matches.

Alan also spotted a hammer he needed near the tools, plus he added fifty mini balls in fifty caliber, a can of black powder, a box of caps for his fifty caliber Hawkins Rife and a box of forty-four caliber bullets for his Colt Revolver.

Beanstalk tallied everything up, two dollars would get it all.

Alan paid the two dollars and Beanstalk put all the items in a burlap bag for him. If he wanted to get food supplies, Beanstalk told him to check with Liam Dobbs next door at the General Store, he might have what he needed. "Also, you said you needed some laying hens, on your way home and about one mile from town, the first homestead on your left is Clyde and Tehya Bolin's place and he should have the chickens you wanted."

Alan thanked Beanstalk for the items and the helpful information and headed next door for his food supplies.

Walking into the General Store he was greeted by the owner, Liam Dobbs with a friendly welcome, "Come on in young man, how can I help you?"

Alan said hello and introduced himself. "I'm Alan Adams and my wife and I just moved into the Smith's place three miles out on Three Bears Trail." He told Mr. Dobbs he wasn't sure of everything he needed, he would bring his wife back later in the week to get more supplies, but for now, he would like a pound of sweet butter and four slices of ham steaks from the hanging cured ham. He continued to look around in the store and grabbed a one-pound bag of salt and two big, sweet onions and asked Mr. Dobbs how much he owed; it came to two dollars for everything.

Alan paid him, and said, "Thank you and it's good to meet you, Sir."

Mr. Dobbs welcomed them to Shepherd Springs, he said, "I knew Fred and Edna well, they were good people and you have bought yourself a fine place."

Alan said, "Yes sir," and walked out, he needed to head home and share all that had happened about his day with Odina, but first he wanted to stop by the homestead Beanstalk told him about on his way to see if he could buy some laying hens.

11. The Closest Neighbors

On his way out of town, about a mile on Three Bears Trail, he could see the Bolin homestead on his left, so he turned and rode up to the cabin. He noticed a man that looked to be in his late thirties or early forties feeding hogs. As he got closer, he said, "Good afternoon, Sir, are you Mr. Bolin?"

Mr. Bolin replied, "Yeah Son, I'm Clyde Bolin and who are you?"

Alan said, "My name is Alan Adams, my wife and I bought the old Smith place."

"Well, we are neighbors then," said Mr. Bolin. He spoke of Fred and Edna, he knew them well, they did some trading and helped each other out when needed and it was sad and odd how Fred died, just in the wrong place at the wrong time.

Alan agreed it was and explained his reason for stopping was to see if he had any laying hens, a rooster and a good milk cow he could sell him, he wanted to buy about six laying hens, a rooster and one milk cow.

Mr. Bolin said he sure did, he had too many chickens to feed and more eggs than they could eat, he had several good milk cows and supposed he could part with one of them. He could let him have the chickens, cow and rooster for about fifteen dollars which was good with Alan, so he paid Mr. Bolin, shook his hand and said, "Thank you, Sir." He would go home, get his buckboard and come back within an hour if that would be okay, but Mr. Bolin said there was no need to do all that, he would have his oldest son Jacob load everything up and deliver it to him shortly.

Alan appreciated the offer and was excited to begin having eggs for breakfast and milk to drink. He left the Bolin's place, headed home to unload the other supplies and tell Odina about his day. As he rode up the path to their cabin, he could see Odina on the porch busy weaving baskets with the wisteria vines she had harvested the day before. She had already made four large baskets and two small ones; she looked up from the porch and could tell by her husband's smiling face he had a good day. She greeted him with a hug and kiss and asked what was in the burlap bag as he was telling her about his meeting with Mr. Stockburn.

He told her the meeting went very well, he was offered the job, he accepted and was hired and would start the next week doing carpenter work since the mining operation would not start for another month or so. He continued telling Odina about going to the Trading Post, meeting Beanstalk and selling the gold for seventy-four dollars to get the supplies they needed. Taking Odina by the hand, they walked inside, he set the bag on the table and began to remove each item. As he pulled out the candles and two packs of long stick matches, he couldn't help but notice the glow on her face. He went on to tell her he spent nineteen dollars of the seventy-four today.

Once the bag was empty, and all the items were on the table, she looked upset and said, "Is this all you got for nineteen dollars?"

Alan laughed as he said, "No, all this was four dollars, but, on the way home, I stopped at our neighbors, the Bolins to meet them and I purchased six laying hens, one rooster, and a milk cow that Mr. Bolin's son, Jacob, will bring to us shortly. I couldn't haul all those chickens on Scout. I paid fifteen dollars for the cow and chickens," and she looked relieved, and excited to have eggs and milk.

He told Odina they had fifty-five dollars left and he thought they should put another ten up for the bank payment, he never wanted to get behind on the payments, so the bank could take their home away from them. Also, he asked her to make a list of other things they would need. "We will go to town tomorrow and take the buckboard, plus, you could take some of your bracelets and necklaces and maybe sell or trade those."

Odina was excited, but concerned the town people would not accept her because she was Indian.

Alan assured her the town folks would love her and there were other Indians in town when he was there. He never noticed any hatred or meanness toward any of them, plus he was half Cherokee and everyone he spoke to was friendly towards him.

Odina took the four cured ham steaks, onions, bag of salt and sweet butter to the kitchen, knowing what she would prepare for supper later.

Alan took all the ammunition and stored it in a wooden box close to the bed and left the candles and matches on the table, grabbed the hammer to hang in the barn, he knew he would need to carry it with him next Monday to use in the carpentry job. Next, he needed to get the chicken coop ready, so he placed some straw in the nests where the hens would lay eggs and found an old shallow pan in the barn that he could put in the chicken pen for water.

As he finished getting the chicken coop ready, he heard someone coming up the path and walked out to see a young man about his age on a horse pulling a wagon with a cow tied to the back. He walked down to meet him and said, "you must be Jacob?"

"Yes, I'm Jacob Bolin and my father said to bring the chickens and milk cow to you."

He thanked Jacob and told him he was ready for them, so Jacob pulled the wagon a little closer to the coop and helped Alan carry the wooden crate full of chickens. They released all the chickens into the pen and took the wooden box back to the wagon.

Jacob told Alan his father sent a bag of laying mash, a bag of scratch feed and a dozen eggs to get him started.

Alan says, "Tell your father thanks for the feed and the eggs, it is very much appreciated," then he took the cow, walked down to the pasture and released it in with the horses.

Jacob looked Indian to Alan, but he didn't ask, and Jacob didn't say, it didn't matter.

Jacob said, "I need to head back now; I have more chores to do before dark."

Alan told him how good it was to meet him, he was glad they were neighbors, and to let him know if he could ever help with anything.

Alan made his way back to the cabin, and Odina was on the front porch finishing up two small baskets, once finished, she would start supper. He was amazed at how talented his wife was. She makes beautiful jewelry and different size baskets out of vines that are useful for many things. He went on inside while Odina was finishing up and put a few of the candles up, so they could use them for lighting. The coal oil lamps they were using made black smoke and smelled bad, so he hoped they would not have to use those much anymore.

Odina came into the kitchen to start supper; she had finished making eight baskets and used all the wisteria vine. Alan had already built a fire in the wood stove, so she took out her cast iron skillet, added a chunk of sweet butter, potatoes and onions, and let it all cook for a few minutes, then added the chunks of ham she had prepared, a little salt and cooked everything together for a short time until it was done. She didn't have time to make flatbread, but Alan remembered he had some in his saddle bag from the morning, so he retrieved it to go with the good smelling meal.

12. Talking to Odina

While sitting at the table enjoying their meal, Alan began telling her more about the day, the people he met and the things he had seen and learned. He told her Mr. Stockburn appeared friendly, an honest businessman and seemed to be impressed with the interview. Next, he met Jack Bennings, at the Trading Post, who everybody called Beanstalk, because he was so tall. He learned a lot from Beanstalk and was amazed at all the stuff at the Trading Post. There was Indian jewelry in a showcase, not as nice as the jewelry she made, maybe they could show him some of hers and he might want to trade or purchase for the store. Next door at the General Store he met Mr. Liam Dobbs, the owner and operator. Mr. Dobbs was friendly and helpful and had a lot of food items and supplies they would always need. Except for Cora-Mae Tibbs, the wife of Nathan Tibbs, the owners and operators of the hotel and dining hall, he met no one else. Mrs. Tibbs took the breakfast order from Mr. Stockburn, and he explained to him who she was. Alan told Odina again she really needed to go with him to town in the morning, so she could meet folks and help him with the supplies they would need; she smiled and agreed to go. After they finished with supper, Alan kissed Odina on the forehead, told her he enjoyed the supper and headed to the front porch to ponder.

Standing on the front porch, looking out across the valley of the Appalachian Mountains, he felt thankful and blessed. As he thought about the things he needed in town, he knew one was a handsaw to use on the lumber, a few pounds of nails, and sweet feed from the livery stables for his horses. Odina would make a list of food supplies to last about a month, they both knew they needed to continue to be careful with their money.

It was Tuesday morning, and they were awakened by the sound of a rooster crowing. Alan yawned and told Odina that was their signal to get up and get busy, the new rooster was doing his job.

Odina headed to the kitchen, built a fire in the wood stove, made a pot of coffee and began cooking breakfast.

Alan headed to the barn, grabbed some chicken feed for the chickens, then back to the barn to milk the cow. He got about a quart of milk the first-time milking; that would be enough for them. He carried the milk to the cabin, poured himself a cup of coffee and went to the porch to admire the morning sun coming up and waited to hear Odina call him to breakfast.

Soon, the call came, and they enjoyed a hearty breakfast of fried eggs, ham and flatbread along with fresh milk.

13. Trading Day

After breakfast, Alan and Odina gathered up the baskets and jewelry, hoping they could sell or trade for things needed, and he headed to the barn to hook Pogo up to the buckboard. They loaded up and headed to town on Three Bears Trail and he told Odina when they got to the Bolin's place, they would stop, so he could thank him for the eggs and chicken feed, and she could meet him and his family. They could see Mr. Bolin out tending to his livestock as they approached his homestead.

As they got closer, Mr. Bolin threw up his hand and said, "Hello neighbor, I see you brought the Misses with you."

Alan said, "Yes sir, this is my wife Odina."

Odina knew that Mr. Bolin could see she was Indian, but he made no remarks except to say it was a pleasure to meet her and then called for his wife to come meet the new neighbors. He called out the name Tehya and right away, Odina and Alan knew that name was Indian. Tehya came out from the chicken coop with a pouch on her apron full of eggs and a young girl following behind her. They could tell Tehya was indeed Indian. She said, "Hello, pleased to meet you, this is our daughter Nova, she is eight years old."

Odina returned her kindness; saying she was happy to meet her and Nova also.

Alan then explained to Mr. Bolin they were on their way to town for supplies and wanted to stop and thank him for the eggs and chicken feed he sent by Jacob yesterday when he delivered the milk cow and chickens and to see if he needed anything in town, they could get for him while they were there.

Mr. Bolin checked with Tehya, and she said they needed salt; they could use about ten pounds and if he didn't mind picking it up for him, Mr. Dobbs would have it at the General Store. He offered the money for the salt, but Alan wanted to wait and settle when they came back just in case Mr. Dobbs happened to be out of it.

Odina dug through her bag of jewelry and found a gift for Nova and asked Tehya if Nova could have the necklace she had made.

Tehya smiled, hugged Odina and told her she would love it.

Odina asked Nova to please accept the necklace as a gift of friendship, the little girls' eyes got really big, a smile came across her face, and it warmed Odina's heart. Alan, Odina, Mr. Bolin, Tehya and little Nova were all smiling.

Alan then told the Bolin's they must be going, but would stop by on their way back.

When in town, the first stop was the Trading Post. He remembered seeing a handsaw in the store and a box of nails he would need. As they walked in, Ole Beanstalk was standing behind the counter, he spoke to Alan and said, "I see you brought the Misses."

"Yes sir, this is my wife, Odina."

"Welcome to Shepherd Springs and my Trading Post Odina," said Beanstalk. He then leaned over to Alan and quietly asked if he brought more gold today.

Alan said, "No, not today, but we brought some beautiful Indian jewelry and a few baskets that Odina made, thought you might be interested in trading or buying some or all."

Beanstalk wanted to see the jewelry, so Odina carefully took out each piece and laid it on the countertop for him to inspect. He was amazed at all of them and thought they would sell, there were fourteen necklaces and twelve bracelets. He then looked at the baskets and said he could probably take two of the large ones and four of the small ones and would pay eight dollars for all.

Alan, being a pretty good trader, asked Beanstalk if he would give seven dollars, the handsaw and a box of nails for it all.

Beanstalk took his pencil to paper and began figuring; he knew he could triple his money on the jewelry and double it on the baskets. He said, "If you throw in two more of the large baskets, I would give eight dollars, the handsaw and a fifty-pound box of nails."

Alan lookcd at Odina, she nodded, "He said it's a deal and they shook hands." He toted the fifty-pound box of nails, and the handsaw to the buckboard. They never expected to have that much money so early in their move here.

Next, they went to the General Store. They noticed a tall lanky gentleman who looked to be in his sixties, wearing a black dress coat, wire rim glasses, a thick gray mustache talking to Mr. Dobbs at the counter. He saw them walk in and spoke to Alan and introduced the gentleman he was speaking with as Doctor Lovie Hogue.

Doc said, "How do you do folks?"

"Just fine, thank you Doctor Hogue," said Alan and he introduced his wife Odina to Mr. Dobbs and Doctor Hogue, they told Odina how pleased they were to meet her.

When Doctor Hogue left the store, Mr. Dobbs told Alan and Odina that Doctor Hogue took care of all the town folks and then some, he was a good man and a very good doctor.

Alan told Odina to let Mr. Dobbs know what they needed, so she gave him her list, ten pounds of cornmeal, ten pounds of flour, ten pounds of salt and a slab of cured bacon. She added two pounds of dried beans and two jars of canned tomatoes she saw on the shelf and asked how much the total for all would be.

He added it up, it came to four dollars and fifty cents for everything.

Alan paid Mr. Dobbs, thanked him and they left the store with all the supplies in the buckboard. As they were riding down to the livery stable, Odina spotted a fabric and sewing supply shop and told Alan she had to go there. They pulled up to the shop, went in and met an old, widowed woman named Martha Baxter who ran the business. Ms. Baxter made quilts, dresses, shirts and aprons while she waited for customers to come in. Odina was amazed at all the fabric, but she would wait to get any, right now she needed some spools of different colored thread. She was able to buy six large spools of assorted colored thread for one dollar.

They rode to the other end of town where the livery stables were, so Alan could get some sweet feed for the horses from Jacob Jenkins. Alan told Mr. Jenkins he needed fifty pounds of sweet feed, twenty-five pounds of scratch feed and twenty-five pounds of laying mash.

Mr. Jenkins helped him load the buckboard and said it would be three dollars.

Alan paid him, shook his hand and said, "Thank you, Sir, I appreciate it."

Starting home on Three Bears Trail, Alan told Odina he felt like they should give Mr. Bolin the ten pounds of salt for the eggs and chicken feed he gave them the day before. Odina agreed they should, he helped them a lot with his kindness. As they pulled up to the Bolin's home, Mr. Bolin walked out to meet them and said, "Looks like you got a pretty good load of supplies in your buckboard."

Alan said, "Yes sir, we are trying to learn what we will need until I get paid from my new job at the coal mine, I even have your ten pounds of salt you wanted."

Mr. Bolin said, "good, how much do I owe you?"

"Not a thing, Mr. Bolin," said Alan, "the dozen eggs and chicken feed you sent to us was enough to call it an even trade."

Mr. Bolin laughed and said, "Alright, but Tehya told me to ask y'all if you would stay and eat with us when you returned from town. She has fried a bunch of fish the boys caught in their baskets this morning, fried some corn fritters and potatoes so y'all can have a late lunch or early supper and it should be ready in a few minutes."

Alan said, "We appreciate the offer and would be happy to stay and eat."

As they sat at the table, he introduced them to two more of their sons. "You have already met Jacob, who is fifteen, the middle one is Ridge, he's thirteen and Lucas, at the end of the table is eleven, 'course you already met our baby girl, Nova, who is eight."

The table had enough food on it to feed an army and there was a small army at the table. Their children were well mannered and sat in silence at the time Mr. Bolin said grace and gave thanks for the food provided and for their new neighbors, Amen. While talking as they ate, Mr. Bolin said he was Swedish and Tehya was Shawnee, so all their children are half Swedish and half Shawnee.

Alan says, "I am half Scottish, and half Cherokee and Odina is Cherokee, we don't have children yet, but we want to start a family when we are more settled in."

After they finished the meal, Alan and Odina both bragged to Tehya about how good the food was and how thankful they were to finally meet them.

Tehya was happy they were their neighbors, and they would always be welcome in their home.

Alan and Mr. Bolin stepped outside to walk and talk while Odina talked with Tehya and helped her wash the dishes. Alan asked Mr. Bolin how much land he had, he said they had a thousand acres with enough game and fish to feed his family. The Red Wolf River ran through his land, and it was the same river that runs just outside of Shepherd Springs where the sawmill and gristmill are located. Alan was curious as to how the river got its name. Mr. Bolin told him the Red Wolf was plentiful in the mountains fifty to seventy-five years ago, but had been trapped and hunted so much they were totally gone and had been gone for fifty years. He never saw one, never heard of one or never even saw any wolf tracks in the fifteen years he had been here, and he had hunted and trapped all over the Appalachian Mountains.

He said, "I may look older, but I am thirty-four years old, and Tehya is thirty and this mountain living is hard, but we love it." They married when he was nineteen and she had just turned fifteen. They first lived on a little piece of land just outside of the Shawnee village where she was raised.

About fifteen years ago, they packed about everything they had and came here to homestead this land and to be blessed with four children; if he and Tehya fell over dead, their children would survive on what they had taught them and that was a good feeling. Alan told Mr. Bolin when he and Odina married, she was fifteen and he was seventeen and now she is sixteen and he is eighteen and they both have the same outlook on life as he and Tehya have. He felt like they were a lot alike even with the age difference and wanted him to know that he and his family would always be welcome at their home as well.

They said their goodbyes to the Bolins, thanked them for an amazing meal and hoped they would be getting together again soon. As they were riding home Odina spoke about her conversations with Tehya. Even though they were from different tribes, their meaning of life was the same and they already had formed a truthful friendship.

14. Exploring

Once home, Alan and Odina talked about the days ahead, he had just five more days before starting his new job and would like to do more exploring of the cabin, barn and their land while he had time since they would need to start preparing for the winter months ahead soon. Getting firewood, hay for the livestock, and canned food stored up would be necessary for them to survive the long cold winter.

For now, he needed to start unloading all the supplies from the buckboard, unhook Pogo from the wagon and put him in the pasture. After he finished, he wanted to inspect the cabin some more. He knew that old timers were secretive and may have several hiding places for their valuables. They still had several places in the cabin and barn to check out. He was in the kitchen part that was added on after the cabin was built concentrating on the food cupboard, and something didn't look right to him the more he looked at it. The cupboard looked to be about eight inches thicker than the shelves were deep, so he pulled on it, slid it out from the wall for a better look when it swung open like a door, it had hinges on it. There was a square hole in the floor underneath and it was smaller than the cupboard and there was a ladder that went down to the hole. He lit a candle, went down the ladder to find what he knew to be a root cellar that had been dug out about eight feet deep, eight feet wide and eight feet long. There were wooden shelves built to hold canned goods plus it could also be used as a hideout if needed. They had never noticed it in the five days they had been there, just glancing at the cupboard, it looked normal. Odina grabbed another candle and went down the ladder to help him look around, she loved exploring also. They found several jars of canned green beans and sweet potatoes on the shelves. It was probably about twenty degrees cooler down there and would serve them well for storing canned goods, cured meats and milk. They were hoping to find another secret hiding place for valuables, but they found no hidden treasures, so Alan thought the hidden treasures that Odina found was probably the only ones in the cabin but, he had not forgotten about the two hand drawn maps he found in the barn with the X mark. Since they had three more hours of daylight left, he wanted to explore more. He pulled out the little hidden box that had the two maps with an X, took the map that showed the X located behind their cabin, and went up to the mountains.

Odina wanted to go with him, so they left on foot since he knew it was pretty easy walking and they might see more by going slow and looking for some kind of sign for where the X would be located on the map.

Alan carried his Colt Revolver with him in case they came upon an angry bear. After hiking for about an hour, they still were not able to locate the X spot on the map yet, but when they went down the northeast slope of the mountain, he heard Odina say Ginseng.

Ginseng plants were covering the whole side of the mountain. They knew the roots of the Ginseng plant were very valuable to some companies for medicinal purposes and it was also used to make Ginseng tea. They looked at each other and wondered if this could be the X mark on the map, finding this much Ginseng would be like a gold mine. They took out their knives and dug enough up to make Ginseng tea. It takes Ginseng many years to grow big roots and they didn't want to deplete their crop, so they only took a small amount. Next time he went to town, Alan planned to check with Beanstalk and see if he bought Ginseng roots or if he knew who did. He was not convinced the X mark on the map was the same location where the wild Ginseng grows, but the sun was going down, so they started walking back to the cabin, he needed to take care of the animals and Odina wanted to make a pot of Ginseng tea.

After they arrived home and the chores were done, Odina fried corn fritters with chopped onions and cooked two small portions of cured ham and made a pot of Ginseng tea. They were not very hungry, so a small supper would be fine, thanks to the big meal Teyha Bolin had prepared earlier.

After they finished supper, Alan headed to the front porch with a cup of tea to sip on while he pondered and listened to the sounds of the Appalachians. Several minutes later, Odina joined him. He told her he was thinking about talking with Mr. Bolin about borrowing or renting one of his mules to plow up the bottom land, so he could plant corn. They could use the corn to feed the livestock, feed them also and maybe sell some to the grist mill in town. There was fifty-nine dollars left to use for necessities they would need for the next month, but he thought they should take ten more out and put it with the twenty they had already set aside for the monthly payment, they would then have three months taken care of, should they fall on hard times. Odina agreed, she wouldn't want to lose their place for not being able to make the payments.

Alan said, "We have the gold you found except the four ounces I sold to Beanstalk, but I rather not sell it right now, I need to check around and see what those beautiful gemstones would bring." He was sure they were valuable, or Ole Fred Smith would not have hidden them with the gold.

The next morning, Alan took Scout, some rope and his ax to look for big limbs laying on the ground. He could drag those back and cut them for firewood. He planned to do a little each day until they had enough stored up for the winter. For the next five days, they continued with their daily chores and gathering other supplies needed. Odina went back to where she found the wild wisteria vines to harvest more for baskets. Mr. Bolin and his oldest son, Jacob, brought two of his mules and helped Alan plant about two acres of field corn on his bottom land.

Alan and Odina tried panning for gold downstream from the fishing hole where they found some dark sand, but they only found a few flakes. That was probably not the best place to pan for gold, but at least they knew there was gold on their land, they just had no time for chasing that dream now.

15. New Job

It was Monday morning, May 10, 1848, and the rooster was crowing before daylight. Today Alan was starting his new job at the Stockburn Coal Mining Company as a carpenter. He was glad he convinced Mr. Stockburn he was a good carpenter, so he could help with the building of the structures until the mining began.

Alan started a fire in the wood stove as Odina put on a pot of coffee and started a breakfast of eggs, bacon and flatbread. He went to the barn and saddled up Scout for the four-mile trip. After breakfast, he had one more cup of coffee, filled two canteens with spring water and kissed Odina bye as she handed him a cloth bag with flatbread and bacon, and he hit the trail. He would rather be early than late, and he was sure he would be early.

When he rode up to the site, no one was there yet, but he noticed a lot more lumber had been delivered. About thirty minutes later, he could see two men coming in his direction, one on horseback and the other in a buckboard that appeared to be loaded down with supplies. When they got closer, the one on horseback said, "Hey there."

Alan said, "Morning Sir."

He introduced himself as Jackson Rakestraw and said Mr. Stockburn hired him as the Building Supervisor for all the buildings they would build on the site. He asked Alan who he was.

Alan said, "I'm Alan Adams and Mr. Stockburn hired me to help with the building of all the structures until the coal mining operation starts up, I will then be working in the coal mines."

"It's good to have you, the big ole fellow on the buckboard is Ben Carter, but everybody calls him Big Hoss and you can just call me Jack."

Alan was glad to meet him and Big Hoss.

Another rider approached on horseback and Jack told him that was Delmar Betts. Delmar owns the carpenter shop in town and was hired to help with the buildings. Jack called them all to the back of the buckboard and showed everybody the drawings of the structures they would build, and the size and locations of each.

Alan saw the buckboard had hammers, nails and saws in the back, ready to use.

Jack explained that before the first could be built, they needed to set up rock pillars for the footings, all buildings would have a shed roof even the shanties. That would make the building go faster and hopefully they could be completed by the time the coal mining started up.

As supervisor of the project, Jack kept a ledger with the names of all the workers and the hours everyone worked. He also made notes of the progress made at the end of each day. The first day was over at four o'clock and they had stacked rocks to form twelve pillars for the foundation and built the floor frame out of big timber. Hauling the rocks from the nearby creek was hard work, but that part was over for that building and Alan was ready for the carpenter's work. Jack was pleased with the progress on the first day and said he needed the first building to be completed by the end of the week. He went to the sawmill every other day and gave Jackson Morris his order for the size and length of lumber needed and every other day, Mr. Morris made a delivery of lumber to the work site.

Alan could tell Jack had done this before and already had many loads of lumber delivered.

When he got home, he had a few more hours of daylight, but he was exhausted from all the heavy lifting and moving the big rocks. He went to the barn first, removed the saddle and bridle from Scout and released him into the pasture. As he walked to the front of the cabin, he saw Odina standing at the front door smiling, she was glad he was home. Alan smiled also, he was glad to be home from his first day and see his beautiful wife. On the porch he noticed four small baskets she had made with the wisteria vines and on one she had sewn beautiful designs in it with the different colored thread she purchased in town.

He walked up to Odina, and she could tell he was tired, she gave him a hug and told him she was making a pot of Ginseng tea for him; to sit on the porch and she would bring him a cup as soon as it was finished. Alan bragged about her beautiful baskets, especially the one she had added in the different colored thread. She planned to use more thread and design the small ones also, women loved to put their valuables in those, and she wanted to give one to Tehya and Nova. The tea was done, and Odina brought Alan a cup and asked about his first day. "It was great; Jackson Rakestraw is my boss, but everybody calls him Jack and two more men work with us. Today was hard, we had to tote a lot of big rocks to form the foundation for the building, but we were able to get it done and tomorrow we will start the carpentry work."

Odina says, "I went to the barn this morning and milked the cow with no name, so I named her Bella."

Alan laughed and said, "Bella it is from today forward, did you name the chickens also."

She said, "Not yet, but they started laying eggs, I got three this morning, and I put the milk from Bella in the root cellar to stay cool."

After drinking the tea, Alan was feeling refreshed and decided he would cut a little firewood from the limbs he brought up yesterday, if he could cut a little every day, he should have more than enough by the time winter came. When he finished the firewood, he went straight to bed and had no trouble falling asleep. Odina wasn't far behind him.

He was up before the rooster and started a fire in the wood stove, excited to start the day. Next, he went to the barn to saddle up Scout while Odina was making coffee and cooking breakfast. While having breakfast Alan asked Odina what her plans were for the day.

She said, "I am going to hike up to the Ginseng crop and harvest some more roots, then ride Pogo to the fishing hole and try to catch a few fish for supper."

Alan said he would try to stop by the Trading Post after work and talk with Beanstalk about Ginseng root and find out if he bought it or knew where he could sell it and how much it would bring.

He arrived at the work site about thirty minutes early and started pulling out the boards that would be used for the floor joists and stacking them closer to the building.

Jack and Big Hoss came riding up and a few minutes later Delmar arrived.

Jack said, "Each joist has to be measured, so I need one man sawing and the other two nailing in place."

Big Hoss said he would do the sawing, that's good says Jack, "We want to try and get all the floor joists in, all the decking on the floor and then all four walls up and secured today, then start the roof tomorrow."

Alan was happy everything was working out great with his new friends, there had been no arguing, and everyone seemed to know what they were doing, even him.

As the day went on, the floor was down, three of the walls were up and braced and Jack said that was enough for the day, they had all worked fast and well together, they would put up the rear wall tomorrow then start on the rafters.

Alan asked if he could have the scrap wood they had left over from sawing for kindling and Jack said sure, "Every bit of it, and that way, all the scraps will be gone." He told Jack he would bring the buckboard every few days and load it up after work.

It was now about four thirty when they all packed up and left work.

Alan stopped by the Trading Post to talk with Beanstalk about the Ginseng root. Beanstalk had bought it before, but it had been a few years, he would need to send a telegraph to a buyer up north and see if they were interested and if so, how much they were willing to pay for it. That way he would know what he could pay for it and still make money.

Alan thanked Beanstalk and would check back with him in a few days. After a week had passed, he stopped back by, and Beanstalk had heard from his buyer who was interested in buying Ginseng root. If he could find someone to sell to, it would change hands maybe three or more times. From what Beanstalk was told, he would be able to pay Alan about six dollars a pound once his buyer confirmed he would purchase, and he reminded Alan it took a lot of Ginseng root to weight a pound. It might take a while to hear back, he would let Alan know when he did.

Three weeks have now passed since Alan began carpentry work, he was happy with the work and wished he could do it instead of coal mining, but mining was what he signed on for. If more building was needed, he hoped they would pull him from mining, either way he had a job. In the three weeks, they completed the storage shed, a small mining office room and one of the shanties. The shanties would be occupied by migrant workers at the mine, and they would build another one soon.

Mr. Stockburn visited the job site to check on the progress and let them know the opening of the mine had been pushed back a month. That was good news for Alan, he loved carpentry. He overheard Mr. Stockburn ask how the carpenters were working out. Jack assured him they were doing well; Big Hoss was a worker and Delmar was experienced by trade, but he was really impressed with Alan. To be such a young man, he works like an older man with experience. Mr. Stockburn was pleased to hear Alan was doing good, he felt better about his decision to hire him. Jack went on to fill him in on schedule. They had started on the second shanty and should have enough lumber on site to build the last two. He asked Jack to get with Jackson Morris at the sawmill and make an order for lumber for two more and to draw up the plans. He wanted the last two larger since some of the migrants had families and would need more room for children. Jack said he would begin working on the plans, figure out the lumber needed and place the order with Jackson soon.

Alan was excited to know there would be additional buildings, it seemed as if they were building another town on the site.

Meanwhile, for the past month and a half, Odina had been busy at home making more baskets and adding designs to the small ones with the colored thread. She also made a fish basket. She had caught several fish and snared a few rabbits to add to their food supply. Each morning, she continued to milk

Bella and gather eggs from the chicken coop.

After work in the evenings, Alan cut more firewood to store in the woodshed. Every few days, he walked to the bottom land to check on the corn which was now about two feet tall and growing well.

He has hauled two loads of scrap lumber home from the job site. The supply was growing, and they needed all they could stock up for cooking and warmth during the cold Appalachian winters.

16. Sloppy Spends the Night

It was Friday afternoon and Alan was home a little early and went straight to the kitchen to see Odina. It was a little too early for supper, so they went to the front porch to sit and admire the view across the valley and talk about their home and how happy and blessed they were.

Soon, Alan spotted a man on horseback going down Three Bears Trail. They seldom saw anyone on the trail, and he was too far away to recognize. He turned and started up the path to their cabin. As he got closer, Alan laughed and told Odina it was Ole Sloppy. It had been almost two months since he had seen him.

Before he got too close, Alan asked if there was enough food to invite Sloppy to stay for supper.

She said there was plenty, and she would add more if he stayed.

Sloppy had a couple of burlap bags strapped behind his saddle but no pack mule this time. "Howdy young man and young lady," Sloppy said.

"Hey Sloppy, good to see you my friend," Alan said and asked where he was headed.

He was on his way to town to see if Beanstalk would buy about two pounds of Ginseng root he had in the burlap bags, he was out of coffee and a few other things.

Alan suggested he stay the night, have supper with them and go into town the next morning after breakfast since it would be late by the time, he made it to town.

Sloppy said, "I sure would not want to turn down a good meal, but I wouldn't want to intrude."

They assured him he was welcome, they had plenty and always enjoyed talking with him and hearing about his good friend, Fred Smith.

Sloppy agreed to stay, he would bunk down in the barn.

Odina made a pot of coffee for the men to sip on while they waited for her to prepare supper.

As they were talking, Alan told Sloppy that Beanstalk might not be able to purchase his Ginseng, he had been talking with him about selling some, but Beanstalk was waiting till the potential buyers could find someone to sell to. According to him, it would change hands several times and everybody wanted to be assured they could sell and make a profit.

Sloppy said, "He either will or won't, but I might have something else he would purchase."

Alan didn't ask what that might be, he was pretty sure it was gold.

Odina brought both men a cup of coffee to the porch and went back to finish frying rabbit, potatoes, onions, biscuits and gravy.

Alan asked Sloppy if he thought Fred ever found gold on this place.

Sloppy said he knew Fred did, but like all good prospectors, he would not talk about the location, and he would never ask him, just like he would not tell anybody if he found gold or where he found it. Fred didn't even tell Edna of all his secret places and all he had found. It could be dangerous if the wrong people found out. Sloppy went on to say there was a lot of Ginseng here, he had seen it while walking through the mountains with Fred. He had talked with Fred about it and Fred had sold some to Beanstalk before, but he knew I would never sneak over here and dig up his just like I knew he wouldn't dig up mine, we had a certain kind of trust in each other, we wouldn't lie, we just didn't tell everything.

Alan then asked about the wolf that helped him find Fred's body.

He told Alan the elders had talked for years about the Spirit of the Red Wolf. They believed that the location of the howling wolf would be where treasures would be found. The treasures could be a place where game could be hunted for food, fish could be caught or maybe where gold and precious stones could be found, and he believed the howling wolf he heard led him to a treasure, his best friend's location. He didn't know if anyone else had ever heard a howling wolf in the area, but he did two years ago and hasn't heard it since.

Alan said, "I heard the wolf howl on the second night we were here, it was a full moon and I walked out on the front porch, looked towards Fred's grave on the hill and saw a wolf standing over Fred's grave just as if he was Fred's protector. It's strange, the wolf left no tracks and there were no signs the wolf had been in the mountains, but it was ghostlike and disappeared as fast as it appeared." Alan said, "I truly believe the Spirit of the Wolf lives in the Appalachian Mountains and Sloppy, Old Friend, I believe you do too."

Sloppy said, "Yes I do, there are a lot of things in these mountains that I believe."

Alan offered Sloppy to put his horse Topper in the pasture for the night where he could graze and have water also.

Sloppy was glad as he knew ole Topper would love it. As Sloppy went to get his bedroll and laid it out for the night, Alan told him he was welcome to stay in the cabin, but if he preferred the barn, there was hay in the loft for a good bed. "The barn's fine," said Sloppy, "I wouldn't feel right in the cabin with you and the Misses."

Alan walked with him to the barn, so he could talk with him more. He wanted to know about Fred's wife Edna and what kind of person she was. Edna, he said was a good woman but more of a city girl than a mountain woman. She made a life here in the mountains because of Fred and they always seemed happy.

Odina called them for supper, she had all the food spread on the table and a chair added for Sloppy. Alan was proud of the great meals she cooked, and this was another great one.

After supper, Alan and Sloppy headed to the front porch to talk. Sloppy had his chew of tobacco and Alan had another cup of coffee. Alan was curious and as they were enjoying the evening, he asked Sloppy, "Did you and Fred ever prospect together or pan for gold on Fred's place."

"No," Sloppy said, "and we never prospected together close to my place, we did pan for gold several miles up the Potomac River, but what he found was his and what I found was mine. It was the same when we trapped together, but never on his place or mine." Sloppy decided to head to the barn, he was full and tired, so time to fluff up some hay and sleep like a bear hibernating.

Alan told his friend to rest well, and they would have coffee and breakfast in the morning before he headed to town.

That sounded good to Sloppy, and he bid Alan goodnight.

Alan thought about the conversation and even though Sloppy seemed careful when talking about Fred, what or where he may have found anything, he learned a lot from just listening to what he wasn't saying.

The next morning, they all enjoyed a hearty breakfast of eggs, bacon, biscuits, gravy and coffee. They talked about the cabin and how well Fred built it, "it will last a hundred years and still be standing strong," Sloppy said. He had helped Fred with the rafters, rocks for the chimney and fireplace, but Fred did almost everything else by himself. Sloppy asked if they had found the root cellar since it was hidden and seemed to be a secret place.

Alan told him they had and asked how he knew about it.

"Well, "Sloppy said, "It was by accident, I came by one day and stopped around back so Topper could get a drink from the trough and the back door was open, I looked in and saw the cupboard was pulled out from the wall. As I walked in, it sounded like Fred had fallen in a well, so I went to the hole in the floor and saw Fred digging and filling up buckets of dirt to pull up with a rope. Fred made him promise never to tell anyone, it was a root cellar, but also a hiding place if needed. Who would have ever thought of putting hinges on a cupboard to swing open like a door and look perfectly normal when closed, Fred was a smart man."

Alan knew It was a great hideout, cool root cellar and a place to hide valuables. Mountain folks are usually trustworthy, but would never tell a best friend or spouse everything about their hidden treasures.

Before Sloppy left for town Alan repaid him for the coffee, he had so graciously given them a few weeks earlier. It was his way of letting Sloppy know how much he appreciated the coffee at a time when he didn't have any.

Alan and Odina watched Sloppy head off to town from the front porch and talked of how much they enjoyed his visit and talking with him. Alan was remembering Sloppy saying the location of the wolf howling was a sign of where a treasure could be found, and the treasure could mean numerous things. The X mark on one of the hand drawn maps he thought might be the spot he heard the wolf howl on their second night here, it was close to the waterfall. The X mark on the other map was in the area of the mountain side where they found Ginseng, but he wasn't sure if the Ginseng would be the treasure. Alan thought since mountain folks, according to Sloppy, would not tell their secrets, he needed to check the root cellar again for secret hiding places as well as the barn and smokehouse. Fred was smart and secretive and could have more treasures hidden here but today is Saturday and chores need to be done before work on Monday. Treasure hunting will have to wait.

It's late Sunday morning and Alan is at the bottom land hoeing corn, and he spots old Sloppy coming down Three Bears Trail. Sloppy rode up and said, "I'm headed back to the mountains, I spent the night at the hotel in Shepherd Springs, then laughed and said I also slept well after a few hours at the Tavern."

Alan said, "I see you still have those two bags of Ginseng root."

Sloppy said, "Beanstalk wasn't interested right now, his buyers are slow on finding a buyer, but I did have something he bought which helped me get my supplies, spend a little time at the Tavern and pay for my hotel stay and meals."

"Now, I'm going deep in the mountains and live off the land for a while but next time I'm through, I'll stop by and check on y'all."

Alan told Sloppy to stop by anytime, he was a friend, and it was always good to see him.

17. Odina is Pregnant

For the next couple weeks, Alan continued with carpentry work. He loved building the shanties and storage buildings, but he knew it was getting closer to when he would have to start mining instead. Four miners had already shown up for work, they were all French and spoke very little English. They would be housed in the first shanty that had four bunk beds, a small wood heater for cooking and heat plus a few things they added to make it more livable inside. The foreman, John Thomas, instructed them to begin opening a section of the mountain where the entrance of the mine would be.

Back at home, Odina had been feeling sick for several mornings and then it would go away, but Alan was worried, so he carried her to town to see Dr. Hogue. After Dr. Hogue's examination, he told her it was not food poisoning, and not a virus. He said, "Congratulations, you are pregnant, and I think you are about three months along" He instructed her to eat well, drink milk, no heavy lifting and get plenty of rest and he wanted to check on her in about a month unless she was having problems. They were very excited to start their family and Alan was sure he knew the exact night their child was conceived. They had made love many times before and after, but he was convinced she conceived the night he heard the howling of the wolf the night his wife was lying in bed waiting for him with the light of the full moon shining through the window on her body.

Now his plans have changed a little and he will need to provide for a family of three. He cut more firewood for the stockpile; it should now last the winter. The corn had tasseled and would be ready to pull soon and looked to be enough to fill up the corn crib.

He stopped by the Bolins on his way home to see about buying more chickens and tell them the good news, they were expecting their first child. The Bolins were excited, and Tehya planned to pay Odina a visit soon and talk with her about motherhood. She had been a midwife many times and delivered several babies and could help if Dr. Hogue could not be there. Alan was so relieved to hear that.

Mr. Bolin said he would have Jacob bring him a dozen chickens tomorrow and they would settle or trade later, nothing to worry about now.

18. Business as Usual

The mining operation had begun and was moving fast. The Frenchmen had already tunneled about twenty feet into the side of the mountain and set braces using large timbers about every five feet for safety issues related to cave-ins. They had struck a vein of coal after they had dug about five feet in. Alan and Big Hoss built a loading dock where the coal carts could dump the coal in a wagon for transport. Mining coal was hard nasty work, but Alan and all the miners were in their element and knew the work well.

It's October now and the mining business is in full swing. They opened two more entrances on the mountain side and are now producing coal out of all three. There are twenty-four miners working in the mines with eighteen living in the shanties and the other six living on the outskirts of Shepherd

Springs. Two of the twenty-four traveled from Kentucky to work and brought their families. They live in the larger shanties since they have children. The eight miners from North Carolina live in two of the smaller shanties and four black freed slaves live in another small shanty as well as the four Frenchmen. All are now occupied and one dollar a month is deducted out of their pay for rent, with the women and children being exempt. Mr. Stockburn also wanted to build a few more shanties for future progress and the foreman, John Thomas, told Alan he would be pulled from mining duties to help build the additional ones as soon as the lumber was ordered and delivered. This was happy news for Alan.

Doctor Hogue told Alan and Odina their baby would be born around the first week of February 1849, so Tehya comes to visit at least once a week to help Odina prepare for the new baby. Odina knew how to sew well making clothes for her family, but Tehya also taught her how to knit, she soon knitted two blankets that would keep her baby warm.

It is cold in the Appalachians now, so they were burning more firewood. Alan continued to cut more when he had a chance, even though he probably has enough already cut. They canned a lot of corn they raised and used the rest to feed the livestock. He spent his time off hunting and trapping, setting his traps on Friday evening or Saturday morning, then checked them on Sunday. If no game was caught, he tripped the trap so there was nothing in the trap when he was working. Alan hunted and trapped to provide for his family but he didn't want to ever waste or take more than they need.

Every chance he had, he searched for the location of the X on the maps. The one where the Ginseng was found may have been just that, but the other location looked to be in the general area of the waterfall and where he heard the wolf howling. He has searched many times for some type of clue.

He and Odina panned for gold in the creek bed and found some gold, but Alan believed the map meant more treasure than what they had found. Sitting on the bank at the fishing hole, he looked up at the waterfall and the steepness of the side of the mountain realizing he had not searched there due to the mountain terrain with jagged rocks. He had already checked the top of the ridge and the bottom with no luck, but he could only search the steep side by climbing and it was too dangerous to do it alone. Odina is the only one he would trust, but she is carrying their first child, and he would never ask her. It could be days before he would be found just like Fred Smith if he were to fall and be injured or killed. He was reminded that Fred was found just a half mile from this location too. His plans were to get a very long rope, go around and up to the top of the ridge, tie the rope to a tree, throw the remainder over the cliff, then repel down and use the rope to climb back up, then search every crevasse in the big rocks that cannot be seen from the bottom or top of the mountain.

Alan arrived back home and began telling Odina that something was telling him to search the cliffs at the waterfall. His plan was to leave in the morning, take about one hundred feet of rope, some matches for a fire to warm by and food. He told her exactly where he would be, and he would be back home before dark. After going to bed, his mind was still thinking about all the signs that told him this could be the place to find Fred Smith's hidden treasure. It could be the location of the howling wolf, the map with an X that points to that area or the creek where they panned for gold which was also in the same area. Alan believed that maybe Fred found something like gold or precious stones and hid them in the cliffs somewhere and to be completely satisfied, he must look in every nook and cranny for something out of place and try to think like Fred Smith since he knew if something was hidden, it would not be where anyone would just stumble across it.

19. Legend and Treasures

Morning had come, it was cold, but Alan was too excited to feel the cold. He saddled up Scout and began his ride to the waterfall. Once he arrived, he tied Scout to a tree on the side of the fishing hole. He went over his route again, he would need to start on the south side where the mountain was not as steep, climb up the ridge then he could head north. He needed to come down the cliff on the northside of the waterfall. With his rope, a burlap bag and a few supplies he might not need, but better to have with him, he started going south at the base of the mountain until he could walk and climb up the ridge. Once on the ridge, he went north until he heard the waterfall below, continued a little further north and started easing his way down to the steep cliff while checking for signs of anything odd that may be an indicator that Fred had been there. After tying his rope to a tree, he stood peering over the edge of the cliff down to the bottom, listening to the sounds of the Appalachian Mountains and hoping to hear the Spirit of the Wolf, but all he heard and felt was the bitter cold on his face from the wind. As he began to descend, he went over a large boulder to a ledge he couldn't see before. The ledge was about one to two foot wide and ran level across the cliff for about fifty feet. It appeared to be a good trail covered with slate rocks and may have been used by wildlife. Looking down, he could see the bottom which would be about a forty or fifty-foot fall, so he held on to the rope a little tighter. He looked across the ledge and saw some large rocks hanging over it, so he knew he would have to crawl on his hands and knees to get very far. Still holding the rope tight, he maneuvered further down the ledge; and at one point, he had to lie on his stomach to get to the rock overhang.

When he made it to the other side of the rock overhang, it opened enough for him to stand. On the left side was a straight drop off about forty feet to the ground, but when he looked to the right, he froze in his tracks, he saw the opening of a cave. Alan thought it could be a den for a mountain lion or a bear could possibly be hibernating in the cave. The cave, from what he could see, was very dark and not knowing how far back in the mountain it would go, he inched closer to the opening with his Colt 44 caliber Revolver in hand just in case there was a bear or possibly a big cat inside. He listened at the entrance for any sounds that might be wildlife and bent over trying to focus his eyes enough to see inside since he wasn't able to stand without hitting his head. Removing the burlap bag from his shoulder, he retrieved one of the candles and lit it to see better inside. With the light of the candle, he was able to go further and could see the end of the cave, it was probably about fifteen feet. Near the end of the cave, he could see some signs wildlife had bedded down. The entire floor of the cave was covered with some type of flat slate rocks, and he noticed a design on the floor that appeared to be manmade. While on his knees, he could not believe what he was seeing. The letter X has been purposely marked on the floor by using slightly different colored slate rocks which made it hard to notice at first glance. Alan was excited and maybe a little concerned as to what he might or might not find. Sitting on the floor at the cave entrance, he listened again for the sound of the howling wolf or a sign from the spirit of Fred Smith. In his heart he knew this was where he was led to.

As he began removing the slate rocks from the floor, he was careful to mark the exact spot where the X was located. Using his eight-inch knife blade, he began digging at the X site and within four inches, he hit something that sounded like wood instead of rock. Alan's excitement began to grow more, knowing if there was wood in the hole, it was put there by man. Upon digging further, he discovered a wooden box buried there and it looked to be about twice the size of the one Odina found in the cabin. Carefully digging around the box, he was finally able to pull it out of the hole. The box was heavy, feeling like it was full of lead and the lid was tacked down. He used his knife to pry open the lid and the first thing he saw was a piece of paper folded, lying on top and several cloth tobacco bags stacked underneath. Alan was nervous, but decided to read what was written on the paper before he opened the bags to see what was inside. The letter read, *if you are reading this letter, it means I am no longer here, and you found the map and figured it out, you found what was hidden. Since I am no longer here, the treasure is yours, be wise in the use of it and it was signed Fred Smith.*

Alan took every bag from the box and laid on the cave floor, he opened one at a time, they were all full of gold. There were eight bags all together, six filled with flakes and two with small nuggets. He estimated each bag would weigh about two pounds or more.

Alan, being a young man in excellent shape and strong, still had difficulty coming down the cliff by rope. Fred Smith was over three times Alan's age so he could not understand how Fred got to this location. It was a good hiding place, no one would ever find it easily, he had hidden his treasures well.

20. Decisions

It's time for Alan to decide, should he leave all the gold for safety's sake or take it back home and risk being robbed? He thought about what he could do with that much gold. He was paid seventy-six dollars for a little over four ounces, but now he has pounds of gold that would be enough to pay off his land, buy more land and still have money in the bank. He just wasn't sure who to trust in purchasing that much gold and didn't know if Beanstalk could afford to buy that much at one time or even if he should try to sell it all at once. He would need to investigate further before cashing in such a large amount.

It's getting late and he didn't want Odina to get worried and send someone looking for him, he certainly would not want anyone to find him and ask questions, so he decided to take two bags with him and leave the remaining six in the box. He buried the box back where he found it, fixed the floor back just as it was except, he left the X mark off. As he started home, he took hold of the rope and peered over the edge of the cliff. The fastest way down was to repel the cliff, but then he would have to leave the rope tied at the top and someone coming by might be curious enough to check it out, so he turned and started climbing back up the ridge using the rope to pull himself up. When he reached the tree where the rope was tied, he untied it, rolled it up and took it with him, he could walk down the ridge and down the mountain side that wasn't as steep.

After getting to Scout, on his way home, he began thinking about Sloppy, and how he spoke of coming by Fred and Edna's place a few years ago when Fred was missing. He hadn't seen Sloppy in several months, but he sure didn't need him to show up at his place and decide to come and check on him.

Prospectors don't tell everything, even to good friends.

When he finally arrived home, Odina was standing on the front porch with a relieved look on her face, she could tell Alan had found something very important by the excited way he looked at her.

As he walked up to the porch, kissed her on the forehead, she said "I was about to send a search party out for you."

Alan said, "I'm glad you didn't, I wouldn't want anyone to know the X location I found."

They stepped inside and he took the two bags of gold out and told Odina they would need to put it with the other valuables in the hidden box. She was excited he had found two more bags, but even more excited when he told her he found a total of eight and left six there in the most perfect hiding place he had ever seen.

Alan went to put Scout up, and Odina went to the kitchen to finish supper.

Once at the table enjoying supper, Alan told Odina how he finally located where the X mark on the map was. He said, "I repelled down the mountain to a ledge and located a cave with a lot of flat slate rocks on the floor. There was a X mark design carefully laid out on the floor and the gold was buried under the X." He explained how hard the location was to get to and he wasn't sure how Fred was able to, but he did and about the note in the box. They both felt sad knowing Fred wasn't here to enjoy the treasures he found but, because of the note he left, they knew the gold now belonged to them. Since this region was not known for having large veins of gold, Alan was shocked at the amount of gold Fred found. He thought maybe Fred knew something other prospectors didn't and that's another reason to keep it quiet. Alan told Odina he would take the bag that he had already sold four ounces out of with him to town and see what Beanstalk would pay and get the supplies they needed.

Odina said, "That is a good idea, I want to buy some fabric and sewing supplies from Ms. Baxter to make baby clothes for our soon to arrive child."

Beanstalk bought almost twelve ounces of gold for two hundred dollars which would get all the supplies they needed, pay Dr. Hogue for all the exams, medical treatments and the home visits he made checking on Odina.

21. Arrival Time

It was the end of January 1849 and bitter cold, but Alan had not missed a day at the mines due to the cold temperatures and snow, the work had just slowed down because of it.

Jack already approved of Alan being off work during the birth of his child, but he couldn't pay him for the days he didn't work. That Alan understood and was fine with it, he appreciated not losing his job for not being there, he wasn't worried about the money, he had saved plus he knew what he had hidden away.

When Dr. Hogue checked on Odina, the first day of February, he told them the baby would arrive soon, but he couldn't stay, he had other sick people to check on. If he was needed during the night just send someone to get him and if not, he would ride out first thing tomorrow morning.

Tehya arrived before Dr. Hogue left and said, "I will stay the night to help in case they need me." She would be happy to help Dr. Hogue. He told Tehya he felt the baby would be born within the next twenty-four hours; he would be back in the morning. Tehya made a pallet on the floor in the corner of the cabin close to the fireplace.

Alan checked to make sure he had enough firewood stored up to keep the fire going and enough to build a fire in the wood stove later so it would be ready to heat water quickly when needed.

The clock on the mantel said eleven o'clock and Alan started a fire in the wood stove in the kitchen to make a pot of coffee. He planned to stay up all night keeping the cabin warm since the temperature outside was in the twenties with a strong mountain wind blowing. While standing in the kitchen, he heard Odina moan as if in pain and Tehya was at her bedside as he stepped nearer to her. He asked if he should ride into town and have Dr. Hogue come, Tehya said there was no reason for him to come and stay the night since he would be back early morning. Tehya assured Alan she had delivered many Indian babies, and should this one come before Dr. Hogue gets back, it would be fine, not to worry.

In between Odina's contractions, Alan stepped outside with his coffee and breathed in the cold mountain air listening to the sounds of the Appalachian Mountains. The moon shaded enough light to make it easy to see the landscape with patches of frozen snow on the ground. Alan stepped back inside, stoked the fire in the fireplace making sure it was good and warm in the cabin since Odina's contractions were getting closer and Tehya let him know it would not be long now, but she was doing fine and excited to have her baby.

Alan had put so much wood in the fireplace, it caught the flu of the chimney on fire. He could hear the roaring sound like a hard wind blowing through a pipe and knew exactly what it was. Stepping outside, he noticed the area around the cabin was lit up like the sun was shining but the light was coming from the flames shooting upward from the top of the chimney. Once the flu got a buildup of soot and cresol, it would catch fire occasionally, they would always just let it burn making sure no ambers landed on the roof or blew to another building and set it on fire. Alan heard someone coming up the path, he saw a horse and buggy and knew it was Dr. Hogue, he did not expect him to be as early but let him know he was glad he was there; Tehya had said it was about time. Dr. Hogue said he could not sleep, he knew the baby would come today, probably early morning and he wanted to be there to help. He told Alan to stay outside for now, he would come and get him shortly.

Alan began pacing back and forth on the front porch while looking towards the heavens saying a silent prayer. The wind had stopped blowing and smoke from the chimney was laying low on the cabin roof making it appear like fluffy clouds. As the smoke slowly drifted over the left end of the roof, it began forming a shape, the shape was of a wolf, ghost-like in appearance but a wolf just the same. Its nose was pointed up toward the stars and Alan again heard the howl of the wolf. The figure of a wolf was frozen directly over Odina's bed and Alan knew his treasure was there. Just then, he heard the cries of a newborn and rushed into the cabin and heard Dr. Hogue say, "Congratulations, Alan, y'all have a beautiful, healthy baby boy."

Alan stood amazed at the two treasures he had before him; Odina was holding their baby boy against her chest with tears of joy running down her cheek.

Dr. Hogue said Odina did great, a perfect delivery. Alan leaned down and kissed Odina on her forehead, wiped her tears away, and told her how happy he was and began to check his son out. A beautiful baby with a set of lungs you could hear a mile away, he was perfect.

22. Naming the Child

Dr. Hogue says, "Alan, go out to my buggy and get my scales so I can weigh this baby boy."

Alan did as Dr. Hogue requested and after weighing him, he said, "this little fellow weighs eight pounds." He wrote the weight on a piece of paper along with the date and time of birth, he planned to fill out the birth certificate when he got back to town, but he would need the name. Alan and Odina had not picked out a name yet since they didn't know if the baby would be a boy or girl. Dr. Hogue asked if they had any coffee.

Alan said, "Yes Sir, I'll get a cup for you."

He took the coffee and pulled up a chair close to the fireplace to warm himself while Alan and Odina discussed names for their baby boy. Odina told Alan she thought his name should be Yano, Alan gave her a surprised look since Yano meant wolf in the Cherokee language. Odina smiled at Alan, "I heard the howling of the wolf as he was being born," said Odina.

"Yano is the perfect name for our son," said Alan, "and what do you think of Phoenix for the middle name?"

Odina loved it so they told Dr. Hogue their son's name would be Yano Phoenix Adams, born February 2. 1849 at approximately five thirty a.m.

Dr. Hogue finished up his coffee and said he would check back in a week unless they needed him sooner. He was thankful that Tehya was there for Alan and Odina, and they were also.

Odina and Yano fell asleep, so Tehya finished straightening out a few things before lying down on her pallet close to the fireplace for a needed nap herself.

Alan lay next to Odina and Yano; the little cabin was full of love and joy thanks to the good Lord above and the Spirit of the Wolf. A couple hours of sleep and Yano woke them all, he was hungry. Odina nursed him while sitting in a chair by the fire and Tehya started breakfast. Alan went to the barn to milk Bella, so they would have fresh milk and check to see if there were any eggs to gather. Yano fell asleep after getting his tummy full, so Odina placed him in the cradle Alan built, and they all sat down at the table for the breakfast Tehya had prepared.

After breakfast, Tehya cleaned up the dishes, straightened up the kitchen and prepared enough food for them for the day. She congratulated them both on their perfect son and how proud she was for them.

Alan and Odina thanked Tehya for her kindness and making the magical event, the birth of their son, so special.

Teyha said, "I will go home for now, but will be back tomorrow morning to help."

Alan was home all day with Odina and Yano. They both were amazed and so happy with their new family member, they couldn't stop smiling.

Alan went back to work at the mines the next day, but every day after work, he hurried home to see the changes in his son. He could not wait till he was old enough to begin teaching him hunting, trapping and fishing.

Tehya checked on Odina every day for the first week, then once or twice a week after that and Dr. Hogue did his follow up visit, Odina and Yano were doing fine.

It was now the end of March and springtime was right around the corner. Alan and Odina had been in their new home almost a year and Yano was almost two months old and really growing. A handsome baby boy with black hair and blue eyes like his father, he was always happy.

23. Tragedy at the Mines

The coal mining business continued to boom, now all three mines were doing well. Alan had been pulled from mining to assist in building a few more shanties for the migrant miners to live in and he was happy to assist, he liked building and working with lumber. He turned nineteen on March 11th and had been working in coal mines for ten years so being able to work outside in daylight was better than being deep down in a dark cave with just a head lamp for light.

Alan was doing an exceptional job working on the shanties and thinking of all the good things happening for the Adams, when he heard a large ground shaking boom that brought him back to reality. He was all too familiar with the sound and smoke that filled the air coming from the direction of the mines. Hearing voices and screams in the distance, he dropped everything and frantically raced to the mines to see workers hovering around mine number two looking down at the large rock, dirt and debris that filled the opening. Alan knew it was bad, he didn't have to ask, he knew it was a cave in and miners were trapped.

The foreman began yelling for everyone to begin digging through the debris and they dug for hours hoping and praying for a sign of life. After taking a headcount, they knew two brothers, Verill and Gabriel Durand were unaccounted for. They were trapped under mountains of debris and the possibility of saving them looked very grim. Alan understood, he had seen it before working with his father in the mines at a very young age. Hour upon hour they dug, shoveled and prayed for a miracle, but as time passed, exhausted, they had to face the fact that time had run out, and the somber reality set in, now it was just a recovery effort. Verill and Gabriel's life had ended in mine number two.

A deep sadness fell over the miners, they were like family with each one realizing it was a hard and dangerous way at times to make a living, but for many, that's all they knew. Mr. Stockburn, visibly shaken, inquired about family to notify but they were from France with no family here and no information on family in France or how to contact anyone.

Alan was very late getting home, and Odina knew something had happened. She was relieved when she heard Alan riding up their path, but she could tell by the look on his face something bad had happened. He looked so tired and was still covered in dirt and dried sweat when he told her they had a cave in, and two miners were killed. Alan told her that all the mines were shut down and all the miners helped to dig the two men out. He also said Mr. Stockburn ordered the number two mine closed permanently and the others closed until after the men's burial. Alan said, the dead were brothers, Verill and Gabriel Durand from France with no known family here and they will be buried in the Shepherd Springs Cemetery tomorrow.

It was decided they would be buried together at Shepherd Springs Cemetery. Preacher John Woods from Primitive Baptist Church spoke at the gravesite and the majority of town folks, along with the miners, came to pay their respect even though most never knew Verill and Gabriel. The women placed flowers on the grave and the town wept for the brothers. Mr. Stockburn directed John to make sure every miner received double pay for the day the mine collapsed and a full day's pay for every day the mines would be closed. At least they could grieve for their friends and not worry about pay. He was a fair man.

After the service, the miners living in the shanties returned home, but their lives were forever changed. It could have been any one of them, the mines were no respecter of people.

Mr. Stockburn told John to put a safety team together to try to find out why the mine collapse happened and what other safety measures could be installed. He pointed at Alan and said, "I want him on the team." John agreed and said he would have three more names by the next morning.

After everyone left, Alan and John remained and began to discuss the collapse. John was curious as to what Alan thought may have caused the cave-in. Alan told him he was thinking the large support timbers were not close enough to shore up the walls and ceiling, but he wouldn't know until he could dig around in the back of the mine. He said, "It could even have been layers of sandstone which is very fragile and will crumble when it's dug into." John told Alan to just meet him the next morning around nine o'clock at mine number two and they would start investigating the cause of the tragedy. Sad as Alan was about the two miners losing their life trying to make a living, he was pleased that Mr. Stockburn had the confidence in him to place him on the safety team so maybe he could help make the mining business safer for all.

Alan left and went by the Trading Post to see if Beanstalk had anything he could get for Odina, her birthday was April 15th, she would be seventeen. He didn't find anything that might suit her fancy, but he hoped, in the next couple days, she would mention something she would like to have.

He arrived home early and greeted Odina and Yano with a kiss, then picked up Yano and walked around bouncing him to see him smile, all the while, talking with Odina about his day. He began telling Odina about being placed on the safety team, they would check all the mines for safety issues.

"Won't it be very dangerous going back into mine number two," Odina asked.

Alan agreed it could be, but they must find out why those two men lost their lives so everything possible could be done to prevent it from happening again.

Yano began to get fussy, Odina looked at Alan and said, "I always just sit in the chair and rock him back and forth for a minute. That always helps get him to sleep."

That would be the perfect gift for her birthday, he thought, a rocking chair, they didn't have one and it would be easy to rock Yano and any future children they had, he would check with Delmar tomorrow and see if he had one or if he could make one ready in the next couple days. He also had ideas on making a small hammock for Yano, it would be good to sit on the front porch, he could nap in it and breathe the fresh mountain air.

Alan arrived at the mines early and talked with Delmar about the rocking chair for Odina.

Delmar said, "You're in luck, I have a really nice one already made and I'll soon finish another one just like it." He told Alan to stop by after work and look at them, he would have the second one finished by tonight, no later than tomorrow night, and if he's not there, see his son Jim. "You can have one for two dollars or both for three."

He then met with John and three others on the safety team. John said the plan was to start the inspection with mine number one first, followed by three and four. They would then proceed to the inspection of number two mine but with extreme caution. They started the inspections and one, three and four were successful, passing all safety guidelines and ready to be reopened for mining. Next, they advanced to mine number two and entered the area where the bodies of Verill and Gabriel were uncovered. First, Alan noticed there were no large timbers used to shore up the walls and ceilings, they would have to carefully dig and remove rocks and dirt to go into the mine further. As they got about five feet further, Alan picked up a large rock, crushed it in his hands as John watched. At that moment, John ordered everybody out. The rock Alan crushed was sandstone which is very unstable when disturbed and it must have been layered deep in the area since there was a lot of it in the rubble.

They exited the mine with Alan explaining his thoughts on the collapse. "The walls and ceiling didn't have big timber support for the last thirty or forty feet and it should be placed every five to six feet, then, if a collapse or cave in happened, there would be a pocket of space underneath that might have saved their lives. He felt the miners were making such good time digging, they either overlooked the safety issue or were planning on adding the support once they were a little further in, but, once they dug under the sandstone shelf, it removed any support holding it up and completely collapsed." John agreed with Alan's findings, he would write up the report for Mr. Stockburn then they boarded up the mine, and marked it, *DANGER, DO NOT ENTER.*

John said, "We are stopping for the day, but be back ready to start mining tomorrow and asked Alan to stay for a minute." He began telling Alan he would like to make him a Safety Officer, he would be responsible for making sure all safety procedures were followed along with making sure the walls and ceilings were shored up the right way with timbers. He would also check the materials the miners were digging into to ensure it was secure, not a dangerous material like sandstone. John said he would ask Mr. Stockburn to raise him another dollar a week, a four dollar a month raise if he was interested in the position. John said, "Before you answer, just know it's a big responsibility and there would be no time for mining coal like you've been doing, you would have to inspect every mine every day."

Alan said, "I am interested, but will Mr. Stockburn approve."

John assured him all the miners liked him and he felt sure they would follow his direction.

"If Mr. Stockburn approves, I am ready to go."

John felt pretty sure it would be approved, but he would know tonight, either way, he told Alan to be ready for work tomorrow, mining, building shanties or performing as the new Safety Officer.

Alan said, "Okay," and headed off to town before going home. He first stopped by Martha's Fabric and Supply shop since she was known for baking and selling very good cakes and pies and he wanted a chocolate cake for Odina. She agreed to bake the cake and it would be ready the next afternoon, he told her he would pick it up after work. Next, he headed down to the carpenter shop, but Delmar had not arrived yet, so his son, Jim, showed Alan the rocking chair. Delmar walked in as he was looking at the finished chair and showed him the other one, he was working on as well, it would be finished tonight.

Alan said, "I will take both and pick them up tomorrow after work." Leaving he was excited to have the gifts on her birthday.

Arriving home, he put Scout in the pasture and walked to the cabin. When inside he saw Yano in his cradle asleep and Odina in the kitchen. He greeted her with a hug and kiss as always and told her he might have a new assignment at work.

Seeing his smile, she said, "What is it,"

Alan said, "They want me to be the Safety Officer for the mines, it pays four dollars more a month and he would know tomorrow if Mr. Stockburn approves."

Odina thought that position would be safer for Alan that working in the mines, she was hopeful he would get the assignment. Alan looked at Yano napping in his cradle, and decided to go to the barn, get the lumber, a rope and a large feed bag to build the small hammock he had thought of earlier. It took about thirty minutes, and he had the stand built, next he cut the feed bag to the right size and asked Odina to sew each end to the round two-foot-long piece of hickory. To finish, he tied each end to the top of the stand, added tanned deer hide to lay on and it was now complete and ready for Yano. Returning to the cabin he took Yano from his cradle and placed him in the new hammock. Yano was cradled deep in the hammock, all smiles, it probably felt like he was floating on a cloud. Even though Alan was still sad over the loss of his coworkers and friends, his heart was full of joy and happiness at this moment with his home and family.

24. New Appointment

Getting ready for work, Alan was anxious and aware today would be the day he would find out if he was the new Safety Officer. He told Odina he would be taking the buckboard today, so he could load up more scrap lumber to bring home from the job site. She would think nothing of it since he had used it many times for lumber, but this time, he needed the buckboard to bring her rocking chairs home.

As he pulled up to the mining office and walked in, John was sitting at the table doing paperwork. When he noticed Alan, he got up and shook his hand and said, "Congratulations Alan Adams, you are the new Safety Officer for Stockburn Coal Mining Company."

Alan thanked John and let him know he would also thank Mr. Stockburn soon as I saw him.

John said, "Mr. Stockburn agreed with everything with the exception of the pay raise."

Alan was silent, but thinking about the four dollars extra a month and what it would have done for his family.

Then John spoke up and said, "He didn't think four dollars was correct, he said to make it ten dollars, so your pay now will be twenty dollars a month."

Alan was speechless for a second, then smiled and said, "Thank you, I appreciate all of the kindness shown to me and my family."

Alan began his workday at his new job as Safety Officer by walking to mine number one and talking to each of the miners advising them to be sure the walls and ceilings were shored up every five or six feet. He said, "If you notice any layers of sandstone, stop digging immediately and come get me."

They all understood and agreed.

The number one mine was in good shape and the miners already had big timbers there to shore up for the next section. He proceeded to mine number three and talked with the miners there, it was not as deep in the mountain side as number one, he noted all safety measures were being followed.

Next, he went to mine number four, he saw the miners had dug a lot of coal out, but had followed all Alan's safety instructions.

After leaving number four, he went to the shanty that Jack, Big Hoss and Del were building. They congratulated him on his new position, he thought John must have told them this morning. He loaded up scrap lumber while there and told Jack he might still be able to help with buildings if needed, he would have to check with the big boss first.

Before leaving Del said, "I finished the other rocker last night, if you still want both."

Alan assured him, he did, he would pick both up after work and go ahead and pay him now. He went into town to speak with Mr. Stockburn and thank him for the position and raise, he would work hard and try not to disappoint him.

Mr. Stockburn said, "Alan, with your knowledge of the coal mining business and your eye for safety, I feel confident you will save lives by enforcing the safety measures." He said, "everybody's goal when running a business or working for a company is to make money, making money and spending money helps everyone survive in the world, but it's always sad when you have workers die on the job who were just working to make enough money to survive on. I like to compensate my workers with an honest day's pay for an honest day's work, even if it costs me more to make sure they are safe at work."

Alan could tell Mr. Stockburn was a good man that cared about his employees, and he was happy he worked for such a man. He walked across the street to Ms. Baxter's shop to check on Odina's birthday cake and it was ready as promised. She hoped they would like it. He couldn't resist, he swiped a bit of the chocolate icing off to taste. "It's so good, Alan said, Odina will love it and little Yano can have a taste also." It's rare for the Adams to have a chocolate cake, this would be a treat. After paying for the cake, he headed to the carpenter shop for the rockers. Delmar was still at the job site, but Alan let Jim know he had already settled with Del for both rockers, Jim helped him load them on the buckboard.

25. Promotion and Gifts

As soon as Alan arrived home, he went straight to the barn and hid the buckboard so Odina wouldn't see the rockers in the back. He released Scout in the pasture, took the box with the chocolate cake and started to the cabin. He couldn't leave the cake in the barn for fear of critters getting into it so he would give it to her now and they could enjoy it after supper. Walking into the kitchen, he handed the box to Odina, "Happy Birthday early, my precious wife," Alan said.

Odina looked at him with her beautiful smile and asked what it was.

He said, "Open it and find out."

She opened the box, "Oh my," Odina said this looks delicious, thank you my sweet husband, we will have some after supper." Her gifts were not over yet, but since he had to work tomorrow on her birthday, she would get them a day earlier. He went to the barn after supper while she was tending Yano and brought the rocking chairs to the cabin and placed both in front of the fireplace.

Odina was so excited over the gifts she completely forgot to ask about his day.

Alan took his son and told Odina to sit in one, he would sit in the other with Yano and tell her about his day. He began telling her about walking into the mining office this morning. "John Thomas stood up and shook my hand saying congratulations Alan Adams, you are the new Safety Officer and he told me what my responsibilities would be."

Odina smiled at Alan and asked if he was happy with the change.

Alan said, "Yes, he was happy." He said he asked John Thomas if Mr. Stockburn approved of the move. John answered yes, he agreed to everything, but the pay raise. He didn't think a four dollar a month raise was correct. Alan paused for a second to look at Odina's face and saw her smile change to a frown. He said Mr. Stockburn said to make it a ten dollar a month raise. My monthly salary now is twenty dollars instead of ten dollars.

Odina was smiling again. She then asked how much the gifts cost. She knew they didn't have much money until payday.

Alan responded, "The price of the gifts was not even close to the value of you."

26. Land Purchase

It was Odina's birthday, April 15th, she was seventeen years old and up early nursing Yano.

Alan built a fire in the fireplace to knock the chill off while Odina was sitting in her new rocking chair in front of the fireplace with Yano, slowly rocking back and forth. Yano would be asleep shortly from the warmth of the fire and having a full stomach, so Alan went to the kitchen to make coffee and breakfast while Odina was tending to Yano.

Soon Yano was asleep, Odina placed him in the cradle, and they enjoyed the breakfast he had prepared.

As they sat at the table, Alan talked with her about cashing in a large portion of the gold and gemstones and possibly purchasing more land. "The government owns the land northwest and east of our property line and he heard talk in town about the government selling the land cheap since it wasn't desirable for farming or building homes due to the steep terrain of the mountains."

Odina was not so sure there would be enough to buy more land, but Alan said, "From what I have been told, it's not good usable land and will be cheap. I will check around town after work to find out more about the land that joins the north border and talk with Beanstalk about selling a large quantity of gold plus find out what gemstones would bring."

Also, he might try to buy a set of scales to weigh the gold himself, so they would know the value of what they had and what they would sell.

Over the next few days, Alan went into town after work and talked with Beanstalk about gold and gemstones.

Beanstalk said the most gold he ever purchased from prospectors was eighty ounces, he paid fourteen hundred or somewhere close to that and he made about two hundred dollars on the purchase, he liked buying gold since it was a quick turnaround.

Alan then asked about the gemstones to which Beanstalk said he would have to see first and check with his buyer before he could give him a price, but rubies, emeralds, turquoise and jade were usually the best sellers since they're used in making all jewelry. He could sell more of Odina's Indian jewelry when she had more ready.

Alan had already noticed most of it was gone from the showcase. He was able to buy a set of scales from Beanstalk. Alan left with the information and stopped by on his way home to check on the Bolins'.

Mr. Bolin told him his oldest son, Jacob, wanted a job at the coal mines and asked if he thought they might hire him.

Alan told him he would check with John Thomas, the superintendent, the next day, but he was pretty sure they would, he would put in a good word for him and stop by on his way home tomorrow and let Jacob know what he said.

As he rode up the path to the cabin, he hopped off Scout and removed the scales from his saddle bag. He could see Odina was all smiles sitting on the chair on the porch with Yano in his hammock. Stepping up on the porch, he kissed Odina, smiled at Yano asleep in the hammock and asked, "How's my wife and son today?"

Odina said, "you know we are blessed and I'm thankful for my hard-working husband."

He sat the scales down and told her he had a pretty good talk with Beanstalk, then he stopped by the Bolins to check on them and about Mr. Bolin telling him Jacob wanted a job at the mines and he would talk to John tomorrow, but he felt they would hire him.

Odina was hopeful they would, they were such good people, but she also wanted to make sure Alan told Jacob how dangerous the job was and to be sure and follow all the safety rules.

Alan assured her he would, then went to the barn, removed the saddle from Scout and put him in the pasture, then back to the cabin for supper. After supper, Alan took Yano to the porch with him and placed him in the hammock and sat down to think while Odina was finishing up in the kitchen. She joined Alan and Yano on the porch when she finished. Alan told her Beanstalk would buy more of her jewelry when she had more made, he had sold most of hers.

Odina was happy people liked her jewelry and she did have more made, but wanted to make more and carry Beanstalk a lot to look at.

Alan thought she might be able to use some of the gemstones and that would make it more valuable, which Odina agreed plus she had ideas on how she wanted to use them. Alan still had an interest in purchasing more land and wanted to talk to Robert Perry, who was the Land Agent for the government about the tracts that joined their property on the north boundary line. Even though most of the land north of theirs was very steep mountains with rock cliffs and would be unusable for farming or living on, he felt that area might hold answers to where Fred Smith found such a large quantity of gold. It was hard traveling in that area, but they might be able to buy many acres cheap.

Alan asked Odina what she thought about selling around five or six pounds of gold, paying off the bank note and checking on buying the land before prices went up.

She said, "It's a good idea," plus, they would still have about ten pounds or more left for financial security.

The next morning when Alan went to work, he talked to John about Jacob Bolin wanting a job with the mining company, he knew him personally to be a hard worker. He had experience in mining coal as well as being a good carpenter which might come in handy.

John told Alan if he recommended him, he would hire him, but he first wanted to interview him, to bring him in tomorrow so he could meet him.

Alan said, "I will, and you will not be disappointed." Alan stopped by the Bolins on his way home and talked to Jacob. He told him if he would go with him tomorrow morning, he would take him to meet John so they could talk, he was pretty sure he would be hired. Alan went over the safety rules and how important it was to follow them. Jacob understood and agreed to always be careful. Alan said, "Don't get yourself killed on the job, I would feel terrible if something like that were to happen."

When Jacob met with John Thomas, he advised him of the jobs he would be expected to do and what his pay would be for a month. When the mines were closed at times, there would be no pay for those days. Jacob understood and told him if given the chance, he would work hard and be safe while working. John told Jacob he was hired if he wanted the job. "Yes, Sir and thank you for hiring me" Jacob said.

After checking on mine number one, Alan went back to the office and John told him he had hired Jacob and wanted him to take him to mine number four to help load the coal carts and push them out of the mine to the loading dock.

Alan sent Jacob into the adjoining supply room to get a head lamp, so he could see deep down in the mine. They would ride the horses to the mine, and he would introduce him to the miners, plus he could do a safety check while Jacob started work on his first day on the job.

Jacob smiled and thanked Alan for helping him get started, he was ready to work.

After checking mine number four, Alan left Jacob with the miners and headed to the building site to talk with Jack. He asked Jack if he needed more lumber from the sawmill, he had to put in an order for large timbers that would be needed to brace and shore up the walls of the mines. He shared with him how well the miners worked together and pitched in to brace the walls as well as extending the rails for the coal carts when needed. They had a good crew. Jack told him he would need more in a few days; he would write out an order. "Just tell Mr. Morris or his brother Larry at the sawmill to bring mine when they bring your order if it's ready."

"I will, said Alan, "I'm going into town and place the order as soon as I check mine number three."

When he finished all the mine inspections and arrived at the sawmill with his order, he talked with Jackson Morris and Larry, they already had what Jack ordered ready and most of what he wanted stacked up and would deliver tomorrow after lunch.

He left the sawmill and stopped by Mr. Stockburn's office to let him know how the inspections were going and assure him all the miners were following his direction on safety steps. Alan then asked his advice on the government land he was interested in that joined his property, he wasn't sure how to go about it or who to ask.

Mr. Stockburn said, "well, the government owns much of the land in the area and he himself leased a thousand acres from the government where they are mining coal." He suggested Alan talk to Robert Perry, the Government Land Management Agent for the area, if he could catch him, he had a little office across Main Street.

Alan had wanted to talk to Robert Perry, he had heard he was the Agent, he just didn't know how to reach him, so he was happy to find out where his office was.

Alan walked across Main Street to the little office, funny, but he had never noticed it before but there it was, painted on the window, Land Management, Agent Robert Perry. When he opened the door and went inside a gentleman sitting behind the desk drinking coffee said, "Can I help you?"

"Maybe you can, if you are Robert Perry?"

He said, "I am, what can I do for you young man?"

Alan introduced himself, "I am Alan Adams, I own a plat of land three miles out on Three Bears Trail and I understand the government owns the land that joins mine on the north boundary, the land is not usable for farming or pasturing livestock, but it would be good for hunting and trapping and I was wondering if the government ever sold land like that and what price it would take to purchase it."

Robert pulled out a large rolled up paper with a map of the area and placed it on top of the table so they could look at it. There were a lot of sections marked government land and he told Alan he must have bought the Smith place.

Alan said he did, the two-hundred-acre section was his.

Robert said, "well, the section joining yours on the north is several thousand acres sectioned off in six-hundred-acre plats, it is very steep with rock cliffs and your entire two-hundred-acre tract is joined on three sides by government land, the north, the east and the southern borders."

Alan agreed, after looking at the map, he was almost surrounded by government land. He was interested in the six hundred acres to his north if it was for sale.

Robert took more papers out of the file to match the numbers on every section. He said, "The government would sell the unusable six-hundred-acre tract for fifty cents an acre, the other sections could be higher, he would have to match the numbers to be sure it could be sold at all."

Alan thanked him for the information and told him he was indeed interested and would talk it over with his wife first.

Robert understood and told him to just let him know.

Leaving Robert's office, he headed back to the mines to check on everyone and let Jack know the lumber should be delivered tomorrow. Since it was almost quitting time, he would check on Jacob and find out about his day on the ride home together.

On the way home, Jacob said, "All the miners were good men to work with and he got along fine with everyone."

Alan, looking over at Jacob, could tell he was tired but still happy, he was proud of Jacob and the good job he was doing, but he couldn't wait to get home and talk with Odina about selling a good portion of the gold, paying off the bank note and buying at least the six hundred acres of government land he had talked with Mr. Perry about today.

Once home, he removed the saddle from Scout, put him in the pasture and started toward the cabin. He didn't see Odina on the front porch as normal, so he went inside to find her holding Yano, singing softly to him while rocking. She smiled as he kissed her on the forehead, looked at Yano in her arms and he began smiling too, they were beautiful. He then began to tell her about going to town to take care of some mining business and speaking with Robert Perry. He said, "Robert showed me a map of the whole area, sectioned off to show what the government owned." He continued to tell her about the six-hundred-acre section that joined their north end, that he could purchase for fifty cents an acre, a total of three hundred dollars. Alan figured they could sell six pounds of gold, pay off the bank note, purchase the six hundred acres and have approximately two hundred dollars left. "We would still have over eleven pounds of gold left with the possibility of finding more on our land. Fred Smith found a lot of gold and it must have been in this area or close by, the six hundred acres may have gold, if we own it no one else could lay claim to it."

Odina was happy with the way Alan had studied the deal and was in total agreement. She had always wanted her family to have a big spread of land and she trusted Alan to make the right decision. Once Odina agreed, Alan planned to go to the hiding place, take out three of the remaining six bags and leave the other three there.

27. **Close Encounters at the Cliffs**

On his way to the hiding place, right before he got to the waterfall and fishing hole, he rode Scout up the ridge of the mountain to tie off the rope, so he could repel down to the rock ledge, this would be a lot quicker and not as tiring as climbing and walking was before. Landing on the rock ledge, he crawled under the rock shelf to get to the cave where the gold was hidden. Standing at the entrance to the cave, he caught his breath and focused his eyes on the back of the cave to make sure nothing was inside, he could sense danger, not from within but above him. Taking a step back, he looked up to his left and on top of a huge boulder sat the largest mountain lion he had ever seen. It was just ten feet above him and appeared to be ready to pounce. As he made eye contact with the big cat, it let out a loud scream that sounded like a woman screaming. Alan drew his Colt Revolver and pointed at the cat, but would only shoot if he had to in case anyone was close by, heard the shot and came to investigate, he just wanted to get the gold and leave. He lowered his gun and stared into the eyes of the cat for what seemed like five minutes. Suddenly, the lion looked to its left, took off and leaped over the large boulders and went completely out of sight. He could hear Scout neighing at the top of the ridge, so he looked to his right and couldn't believe what he saw, the image of a very large wolf, with its head pointed to the sky and howling. Getting a better look at the wolf this time, it didn't appear to be ghost like in appearance like the times before and he knew the wolf had scared the mountain lion off. The wolf disappeared quickly, but he felt sure, this time, he would be able to find its tracks at the spot where it was standing. All was calm now on the ridge, Scout had stopped neighing, so he collected the three bags of gold and buried the remaining three. Once he reached the top of the ridge, he untied the rope, checked on Scout and walked about fifty yards to where he saw the wolf. Alan was a very good tracker, one of the best, but there was no sign the wolf was ever there and no tracks either. He truly believed it was the Spirit of the Wolf that frightened the mountain lion away and he was thankful his protector was there to keep him safe.

28. Paradise gets Larger

Alan and Odina weighed a total of six pounds of gold which at eighteen dollars an ounce, should bring seventeen hundred and twenty-eight dollars. They should owe eleven hundred thirty dollars on their land after subtracting the payments already made. After paying the bank off and buying the six hundred acres for three hundred dollars, they should have two hundred ninety-eight dollars left to purchase additional land or supplies needed.

Odina said, "You sure are good with figures, you can make it work."

Alan laughed and told her she wasn't the only smart one in school.

Over the next couple weeks, Alan sold a little over six pounds of gold to Beanstalk, paid off the banknote and received the deed for their property. Then, he talked with

Robert about purchasing the six-hundred-acre tract that bordered his land. Robert told him it would have to be surveyed again, the boundary lines marked, and he would have to pay the thirty-dollar surveyor's fee, so the total cost would be three hundred thirty dollars.

Alan agreed and would pay once it was surveyed and marked.

The survey was completed within a few days and Alan paid the survey fee along with the cost of the land, they now owned a total of eight hundred acres and still had eleven pounds of gold with the chance of finding more. His job with the mining company was secure, he had a steady paycheck, and he loved his job.

Every morning when he left for work, Jacob was waiting for him on Three Bears Trail to ride to work with him. Alan was proud of Jacob and enjoyed hearing about how he was doing but always reminded him to be safe. There was only a three-year difference in their age, and Jacob reminded him of his younger brother Mato, he was seven and Alan was ten when he drowned nine years ago. Mato and Jacob would be the same age and that's why Alan felt so close to him.

For the next few weeks Alan was able to do more exploring on the new land and found many things of interest. He found another large creek running through the upper section of the property and some deep holes good for fishing. On the east side of the mountains, he located more Ginseng plants in a large area. There were a lot of deer and squirrels that would provide food for the family. He saw signs of bears, mountain lions and bobcats but no wolf signs. Alan had heard the howling of the wolf about three times since they moved here in April 1848. He had seen the ghost like image three times also, but the Spirit of the Wolf leaves no signs to see and very few have heard the howling or seen the wolf.

Fred Smith's camp and the place where his body was found is on the new land. Most of the mountains were very steep, which made traveling hard, but Alan thought Fred knew something special about this area and he needed to think like Fred. Things just didn't add up and he wondered if Fred came to this area because he found gold and then used trapping as a decoy in case someone came through here, he didn't believe Fred was just hunting and trapping, especially since a large amount of gold was found hidden on Fred's land. He felt sure the gold Fred found was on the six hundred acres and he probably took it back to his land to hide, a good prospector would never hide his treasure where he found it. Alan recalled seeing some traps hanging on a tree and finding the pans used for gold when he first found Fred's camp. There was a shovel that could be used in a cave in the tight quarters. Maybe Fred would set a few traps for foxes and bobcats to have pelts to show when he returned home, but after the traps were set, he would go to his secret place to dig and pan for gold. He would search more as he had time, but he needed to continue working at the mines and working around their home. Owning this land, he believes, is just as good as money in the bank, but they already have enough gold to last them for years.

29. Yano turns Four

It was January 30, 1853, and they had accomplished more than they ever could have imagined in the last four years. The greatest treasure was Yano, he would be four in three days. Alan carried Yano with him whenever he went exploring and had taught him to identify the different tracks they saw, Yano loved to go and tell his father what animal made the tracks. While planting corn on the bottom land, he explained to Yano the importance of growing your own food, how to fish and how to swim in their favorite fishing hole. He was very proud of Yano; he had learned so much at such a young age.

Alan arrived home from work on Yano's birthday with a few special gifts for him, a small chocolate cake Ms. Baxter had baked, and a wolf he carved out of wood for Yano to have as his protector. Yano had been riding Odina's horse PoGo bareback by himself for the past year, so Alan felt he needed his own, he would teach him how to care for it. He bought a beautiful light gray horse with a dark gray tail and mane from Jacob at the livery stable. He put Yano's horse in the barn and left the carved wolf on the porch for a surprise later while carrying the cake in, and Yano's eyes got really big, he had never had a chocolate cake.

It thrilled Odina that Alan thought of the cake, and they would enjoy dessert after supper. Then, he told Yano to get the fancy piece of wood from the front porch and bring it to him.

Yano came in all excited, "It's a wolf," he said.

Alan said, "Yes it's a wolf Yano, it is your protector, put it over your bed in the loft."

They could not figure out how he knew it was a wolf, he had never seen one.

Odina was starting supper, when Alan asked her to wait a few minutes, he wanted her and Yano to come with him to the barn. Odina was puzzled, but was sure it was going to be another surprise.

As they approached the barn, Odina saw the beautiful gray horse in the stable, Yano had not seen it yet. She looked at Alan and whispered, "Where and how did you get that horse?"

Before he could answer, Yano spotted the horse and asked if he could ride him.

Alan said, "Yes, you can, but only for a few minutes, he's yours, you have to name him and take care of him."

Yano said, "I will take good care of him," so Alan put the bridle on and helped Yano up and off he took riding bareback.

Odina was so proud for him to have his own horse, and even though he was young, he would learn the responsibilities of caring for livestock.

Alan, with his arm around Odina watched their young son ride bareback like a pro and he could tell she was okay with his decision.

After a few minutes, he told Yano to come back to the barn, time to get ready for supper.

Yano asked if he should put Smokie in the barn, the pasture or stable.

Alan smiled at Odina and said, "I guess he has named his horse Smokie," and they both laughed. Alan said, "Put Smokie in the stable for tonight, give him sweet feed and I will help you get some water, but at the same time, cautioned him never to ride unless he was home from work, so he could be with him. He understood Yano was just a young boy and could not be expected to be more now, but from what he had already learned, by the time he was ten he would be able to survive if he ever got lost in the mountains. Every time they were together, he taught him more about hunting, trapping, fishing and about the plants, the berries, and what was safe to eat, shelter from the cold and how to build fires for warmth.

Odina, on the other hand, was teaching him about chores such as gathering eggs, bringing in stove wood and water from the spring. They both would teach him the Cherokee language, heritage and respect for the land.

At four years old, Yano obeyed his parents most of the time, except for when he wandered too far from home while investigating his surroundings. He was excited to be given chores, especially gathering eggs. It was funny to Yano when he dropped one, it cracked open on the ground and the chickens rushed in to eat it up fast. His mother scolded him, and told him to be careful, that was their food he let the chickens eat. At first, what he thought was funny, he realized and understood after being scolded, it wasn't.

30. The Ghost Deer

Since Yano inherited the joy of exploring from his parents, as soon as he finished his daily chores, he continued to explore close to the cabin and always under the watchful eye of his mother. One day he ventured further than normal, behind the cabin toward the mountain, further than he had gone before. He saw rabbit tracks, deer tracks and looked up to see blackberries, he remembered his parents telling him they were good to eat so he began picking berries.

With stains on his lips and hands, he was enjoying the treat. When he looked over the blackberries, he saw several deer at the base of the mountain close to the freshwater spring, so he stood perfectly still, so as not to spook them. While watching, one stepped out from behind the brush, the deer looked like a ghost, it was mostly white, not the same color of brown as the other feeding deer and Yano was frightened. Once they smelled the scent of Yano, they took off and were gone in a second.

Yano was so scared, he began running back to the cabin where Odina was in the back yard washing and hanging clothes, she saw Yano running toward her and thought something was chasing him, he looked so scared. She ran into the cabin, retrieved the Hawkins Rifle and ran to meet him with plans to stop whatever it was. As they got closer to each other, Odina could see Yano from a distance, and it looked to be blood all over his mouth and face. She ran faster to get to her son only to see nothing was chasing him and what she thought was blood was blackberry stains. She asked, "What frightened you Yano?"

With big eyes and out of breath he said "deer, ghost deer."

"What do you mean ghost deer?" said Odina.

He told her there were many deer, but one was white like snow and looked like a ghost.

Odina calmed him down by telling her young son what he saw was not a ghost deer, but a rare color known as Piebald deer. She went on to explain to him if you see a Piebald deer in the wild it means change is coming and you are forbidden to kill one, "Do not fear the deer, but respect it. Most people go their entire life and never see one, you must be very special Yano."

He understood, looking up at his mother with his blackberry-stained mouth, he vowed never to kill a white deer or be afraid of one. Walking back to the cabin Odina asked Yano if there were any blackberries left or if he ate them all.

Yano said when he saw the white deer he forgot about the berries, he thought there were some left.

She laughed as they entered the cabin. She knew seeing a Piebald deer meant change was coming, which could mean good or bad, but she's pretty sure it would be good; she needed to visit with Dr. Hogue to confirm it.

When Alan came home from work, Yano ran to the barn to greet him and ask if he could ride Smokie as he did every day. This time he also wanted to tell his father about the white deer he saw. As Yano began to tell him about exploring and all he saw, Alan stood listening to the excitement in his young son's voice. He continued to tell him all the details of seeing the animal tracks, the blackberries and what he thought was a ghost deer and how scared he was. Yano said, "Mother told me it wasn't a ghost deer, but a very special deer that I should not be afraid of or ever kill, and to always respect it."

Alan said, "Your mother is right, let's go to the cabin, we will ride Smokie later."

31. Change is Coming

Odina greeted her men at the door with a smile as she normally did, but Alan noticed her smile seemed to be different, more like a radiant smile, instead of her usual smile he saw when he came home from work. She asked if Yano had told him what he saw today.

Alan said, "Yes, he did, he was really excited, did you see the deer also?"

"No, but it must have been a Piebald deer," they both agreed it meant change was coming which could be good or bad.

Alan looked at Odina with a puzzled look and said, "You greeted me this afternoon, your smile was beautiful as always, but there was a different beauty to it, almost like you might know something about the change that is coming."

Odina told him she was going into town tomorrow and see Dr. Hogue to confirm what she already knew.

Alan asked what she meant, and she replied, "Yano would soon have a younger brother or sister and the change would be good for him because he saw the Piebald deer." Alan was so happy, he hugged Odina, they both wanted more children and now they were settled in, in good financial shape, it would be great for Yano to have a sibling to grow up with.

The population of Shepherd Springs was growing, it had increased from sixty in 1848 to one hundred twenty in 1853 and according to Dr. Hogue, it would increase around the first week of July. A lot of people came to Shepherd Springs to work in the mines and others to open new shops in town. The hotel added six more rooms and hired more people, the Morris brothers hired four men at the sawmill due to increased demands for lumber and Ms. Baxter added a bakery shop to the fabric and sewing supply shop. Marshal McCall hired two more full time deputies and the stagecoach now stopped every three days.

In the past five years, Alan and Odina, through hard work and luck, had accomplished so much for a young couple. They were teaching Yano, mostly by home schooling, the Cherokee language, English, arithmetic, reading and writing along with nature and how to survive off the land should he ever have to.

Alan had enclosed the left side of the cabin making two small rooms, one bedroom for him and Odina and the smaller bedroom for guests or additional children later. Yano had made the loft his bedroom.

Alan continued to search their land when time permitted and made trails throughout the eight hundred acres. He found a natural lake on the northeast end of the property, about three acres in size with crystal clear water and great fishing. He built a small shack at the lake for a place to stay when hunting, trapping or fishing in the area. At times when he could hunt and pan for gold, he found several sites, one at Fred Smith's old camp, the base of a steep rocky mountain with a spring coming out of the mountain and at the lake where he built the shack. He found enough gold in the three locations to know it was there for the taking when needed, but he would only tell Odina and caution Yano the importance of not speaking of finding gold to anyone due to the dangers of being robbed. Alan still had not found the location of the X on the second map that could be another location where treasures would be found unless it turned out to be the wild Ginseng root, he still wasn't sure. Working full-time for the Stockburn Mining Company and completing chores at home, didn't leave a lot of time for searching but if there was something there, he was sure he would eventually find it.

32. Falling on Hard Times

Jacob was doing well at the mines and now had a wife, he married one of the coal miners' daughters. He and his wife, Sarah, moved into one of the shanties at the mines and Sarah began working at the hotel for Mr. and Mrs. Tibbs, cleaning rooms, washing dishes, helping with cooking, and serving meals to the customers.

Clyde in the meantime broke his right leg and left ankle when a four-hundred-pound hog ran into him, and Dr. Hogue said it would be at least two months before he would heal enough to walk.

While Tehya and Nova were working around the house feeding the livestock, and gathering eggs to sell in town, Ridge and Lucus were doing all they could to keep the farm operational. Mr. Bolin was bedridden, and they were taking care of him as best they could.

Alan stopped by every day after work to help his sons with the chores and found out they were on the verge of losing their home, they were five hundred dollars behind on payments and had already received two extensions, they had three days to pay or leave.

When Alan finally got home, he told Odina what he had learned about their neighbors being behind on the payments and would soon lose their home if five hundred dollars wasn't paid in three days. He knew there was no way they could come up with that amount of money, Mr. Bolin was bedridden and couldn't work, Jacob had married and moved out and it wasn't possible to sell five hundred dollars' worth of eggs in three days. Odina felt like they should help, and Alan agreed, the Bolins had always been good and quick to help them whenever they needed help, they had to return the favor, besides that, they didn't want to lose the best neighbors they had.

Alan set the scales he had bought on the table, retrieved a bag of gold from their hiding place, he needed to weigh twenty-eight ounces, he knew that would bring five hundred and four dollars.

The next morning, he carried thirty ounces with him instead of twenty-eight to sell to Beanstalk. The extra would buy food supplies for the Bolins. Taking a break at lunch, he went directly to the Trading Post and Beanstalk was happy to purchase his gold. After weighing, Beanstalk confirmed it was thirty ounces and paid Alan five hundred and forty dollars. He thanked Beanstalk and headed to the bank to meet with Mr. Barber.

Upon entering the bank, Alan was greeted by the Assistant Teller, Mr. Theodore Baker, who told him Mr. Barber went to the dining hall to eat and should be back any minute. Alan decided to wait, the business he needed to handle was with the bank. About three minutes later, Mr. Barber walked in and saw Alan waiting. "Hello Alan, how are you today?"

Alan said, "I'm fine Mr. Barber, but I need to talk with you about helping out my neighbor."

Mr. Barber hung his head down and asked if he meant the Bolins, they had had a hard time lately, had been given two extensions and the Land Management Company would not give any more.

Alan assured him he understood, but he was there to pay the back payments.

Mr. Barber said, "That's very noble of you, but the amount owed is close to five hundred dollars."

Alan asked him to look it up and give him the figure.

He pulled the paperwork out of filing cabinet; the balance was four hundred eighty dollars.

Alan said, "That's fine, tell me what the amount will be if you add the next two months?"

Mr. Barber figured again, the total would be five hundred twenty dollars, which would cover the back payments and the next two months in advance."

Alan paid Mr. Barber and watched as he updated the contract to show it was paid up to date and two months in advance. He agreed with Alan the Bolins were some of the towns best citizens and he was a good man and friend to do that for them. Alan said, "When we first came to town as complete strangers, Clyde and Tehya helped us in many ways without question and this gesture is small in comparison to what they have done for us." He thanked Mr. Barber and headed to the General store.

At the General store, he gave Mr. Dobbs a list of what he wanted, paid him and told him he would stop by after work and pick the items up if that would be okay.

"That will be fine," said Mr. Dobbs, "I'll see you then."

He left and went back to work to finish the day. Once there, he checked on Jacob then completed inspections on two more mines.

Alan finished work and stopped by the store to pick up the food supplies and bought a couple pieces of beef jerky to snack on while on his way home. He stopped by the Bolins to drop off the supplies and check on Mr. Bolin and he saw Dr. Hogue's horse and buggy out front. Tehya met him at the door to let him know Dr. Hogue was with Clyde, he had pneumonia. The news upset Alan, but he didn't let Tehya know. He told her he brought some food supplies for them so they wouldn't have to worry about that with everything else that was going on. A slight smile came over her face, with a tear in her eye she thanked Alan, she was out of the supplies he brought. Alan pulled Tehya off to the side, so Mr. Bolin couldn't hear and told her the back payments on their land and two months in advance had been paid, they didn't have to worry about losing their home. She began to cry and said, "I don't know how we can every repay you for such an act of kindness."

Alan said, "Y'all already have, by the help you've been to us." He felt good knowing this would help them greatly.

Dr. Hogue was at Mr. Bolin's bedside and Alan watched as he tilted Mr. Bolin to his side and started tapping him on the back with a cupped hand for about ten minutes. He heard Dr. Hogue tell Mr. Bolin he wanted him to sit up as much as possible several times a day and cough as hard as he could and if he had any Ginseng, make tea and drink it as well at least a couple times a day. Tehya heard Dr. Hogue, but she said they didn't have any and couldn't afford it now.

Alan said, "You will have some shortly."

As he was leaving, Alan saw Ridge and asked him to come with him and help dig some Ginseng, so his dad could have tea to help with the pneumonia.

Ridge said, "Yes Sir, let me get my horse."

They rode to Alan's place, he told Ridge to go to the barn, get two shovels, an empty feed bag and come to the cabin. Alan went inside and told Odina what he was doing and would tell her the rest later.

She smiled and said, "Okay, you both go ahead." They rode the horses to the Ginseng patch and were able to dig up a lot of Ginseng roots that should last a good while. Ridge knew what Ginseng looked like, but never saw any on his family's land and was amazed at how much was there. Alan cautioned Ridge not to tell anyone, especially strangers, about the patch, it was valuable, and the wrong people might try to steal it. He said your family was welcome to it, just let me know first and I'll help you dig it up.

They rode back to the cabin and Ridge left for home with the Ginseng roots; his mother could now make tea to help his father heal.

Alan told Odina about selling the gold, paying the past due payments of the Bolins and paying two months in advance. He also bought flour, cornmeal, salt and a slab of cured bacon for them.

Odina was proud of him for being so thoughtful in helping their good friends that did so much for them and Alan said he was just happy they were able to help them, it's a great feeling to which she agreed.

The next day after work, Alan stopped by to check on Mr. Bolin and see if the boys needed any help with the chores. Dr. Hogue was back again tapping on Mr. Bolin's back as he did the day before. Tehya took Alan to the beside of Mr. Bolin, so he could talk with him. Alan asked Dr. Hogue what tapping on his back would do and he told him it would help break the mucus loose from the lungs and allow him to cough it up and make breathing easier. Tehya said he seemed a little better today and she was sure the Ginseng tea helped along with the treatments from Dr. Hogue. Mr. Bolin's left ankle had healed enough to put a little weight on it, but his right leg had not. Dr. Hogue said he would come by again tomorrow to check on him and he would bring crutches, they would help him get around some in the house, then in a few weeks he could start putting some weight on his leg.

After Dr. Hogue left, Alan sat down in the chair beside his bed. Mr. Bolin told him he really appreciated what he had done for his family, so they could keep their home, he felt terrible about getting in bad shape and not being able to make his payments, but he could now see light at the end of the tunnel and knew everything would be alright thanks to him.

Alan said, "Mr. Bolin, you and Tehya helped me and Odina so much when we were strangers to y'all, we couldn't have made it work without your help and we will forever be grateful to you both."

Mr. Bolin said, "Alan, it's about time you call me by my first name, I know it's out of respect that you call me Mr. Bolin and I appreciate that, but friends call friends by their first name."

"Okay Clyde, it is my friend," Alan said.

33. More about Sloppy

When Alan got home, Yano ran out to meet him asking if he could ride Smokie.

Alan told him in a few minutes he could, but first he wanted to check on his mother. He went up to the cabin to check on his beautiful wife that was with child and see how she was feeling.

Odina said she was fine, just a little morning sickness, but it didn't last long, and she was feeling so blessed they could live in their own little paradise and help their friends also.

He and Yano were going to ride a little while, but would be back in time for supper.

Odina said, "You men go ride, have fun and don't explore too much."

Alan told Yano he would ride PoGo bareback just as he will ride Smokie, so he removed the saddle from Scout and put him in the pasture.

As they rode off, Odina was standing on the front porch watching a father and son riding off together and her heart was full. During the ride, Alan was teaching Yano about different kinds of trees, and the kind of tracks they saw. He understood that young children will remember a lot of things if you don't overload them with too much information at one time, but he enjoyed spending time with his son and teaching him about life. Once at the fishing hole near the waterfall, they dismounted and walked down to the sandbar. He pointed out fresh bear tracks to Yano, it seemed the bear visited the area often.

Alan explained to Yano how he could tell the tracks were fresh and it would probably be the same bear leaving the tracks. While at the fishing hole, he told him the many things available there to use as bait for the fish, he just had to look.

Yano listened to everything; he was eager to learn from his father.

Alay said, "It's time to start heading back, I don't want your mother to be upset with us." They mounted up, rode down to the west corner and cut across to Three Bears Trail on the way back to the cabin. He was proud of the way Yano rode, he rode as if he had been riding for years, he could hop off Smokie fine, but still needed something to stand on to mount.

Riding down the trail, Alan saw a lone rider ahead of them and he recognized the very first friend he made when they moved here, it was Ole Sloppy who he had not seen in several months.

Sloppy heard the horses behind him and stopped to wait, he knew it was Alan.

"Where you headed old friend?" Alan said.

Sloppy laughed and told him he was on his way to town; he was out of coffee.

"Why don't you come and have supper with us, we have coffee and Odina will be happy to see you"

"I built a small bunkhouse next to the barn, you could stay the night and put Topper in the pasture with the other horses."

Sloppy said, "If you keep spoiling me, I might not ever leave, I could never turn down a meal Odina prepared, thank you for the invite, I would love to stay the night and go into town tomorrow morning."

Alan told Yano to ride ahead and let his mother know an old friend would be joining them for supper. He was happy Sloppy agreed to stay the night, he learned a lot from his old mountain friend and enjoyed hearing more about Fred Smith.

They arrived back at the cabin, and Odina greeted them from the porch telling Sloppy how good it was to see him.

Alan told her he would be spending the night with them in the bunkhouse.

She said, "Come back to the porch after you put the horses up and I will have a pot of coffee waiting for you while I finish supper."

When they returned to the porch, Odina brought a pot of coffee and two cups, as the elders talked, Yano sat on the floor facing them listening carefully. He was about to interrupt when Alan looked at him, shook his head and Yano understood and remained quiet.

A few minutes had passed, and Alan asked him if he had something he wanted to say to Sloppy, he could speak now, but he was never to interrupt his elders while they were speaking.

Yano told Sloppy about seeing a white ghost deer.

Sloppy said "You did? The white deer is not seen by everyone, they are very rare and if you see one it means change is coming, it carries a powerful spirit, and you are forbidden to kill one."

He went on to tell him how afraid he was at first, but his parents told him the white deer was not to be feared.

Odina stepped out on the porch and called for Yano to come in so the men could talk.

Alan said, "I see you are still hauling the bag of Ginseng root with you."

Sloppy said, "Yes, I will try to again to sell it to Beanstalk, but if he doesn't want it, I have something else he will always buy."

Alan knew he was talking about gold and didn't want to ask, but Sloppy volunteered saying he had been prospecting since he last saw him. He had found a fair amount and intended to sell about two pounds; most were small nuggets. "I can get the supplies I need from the sell and visit Roosters Tavern for a few good shots of whiskey and buy a couple bottles to have at my cabin for special occasions."

Alan was curious, "What special occasions?" he asked.

Sloppy laughed, "when it rains or doesn't rain, when it snows or doesn't snow, when the moon is full or when it's not full, but my favorite occasion is when day turns to night."

They both laughed and enjoyed sharing in the humor. Then Alan told him about purchasing six hundred more acres of government land that joined his north boundary.

"I hope you didn't pay too much for it, it is mostly steep mountains with rock cliffs and the government knows it's not suitable for farming or mining coal, but they don't know of hidden treasures land like that could hold," said Sloppy.

Alan agreed, they didn't know, and he wasn't going to tell them. He told him about the natural lake at the northeast corner, how beautiful it was, it had the best fishing, and he built a small hunters shack he could use when he had time to hunt, fish or trap, but there wasn't much time with working full time and doing the work needed at home.

Alan was honored to have Sloppy as a friend, but told him he was concerned that he had no idea how to find him if he was ever in trouble or sick.

Sloppy laughed and said, "Walk with me down to Three Bears Trail and I'll show you something I've never shown anyone except Fred."

Alan knew then he had gained Sloppy's trust. Once on Three Bears Trail, he pointed to the mountains that sloped down to the right, then said, "look at the mountain behind that mountain where it slopes down to the left, there is a narrow valley that runs west between the two mountains, that is how you would get to my place."

"Is that where you cabin is?" Alan asked.

He said, "No, that is how you have to travel to get to it, it's rough traveling in the narrow valley and dangerous, but when you reach the area where the mountain in the back slopes down to ground level, you will see two separate stacks of big rocks, turn to your right at the rocks and go three more miles to my place, if you are a good tracker, you could find me, but I trust you enough to never tell anyone. Whenever I have a couple days to spare, I will take you to my cabin, so you will know for sure."

Alan thanked him for placing his trust in him vowing never to tell anyone.

After supper, they went back to the front porch to talk more and he shared with Sloppy how well his job at the mines was going, he loved working there and he made a good living, he planned on working there until the coal ran out or the mines closed and if that happened, he knew how to live off the land and he would enjoy doing that as well. Alan asked Sloppy if it was hard giving up a steady payday and becoming a mountain man living off the land completely.

He said, "I have never regretted my decision, the mountains have so much more to offer if you know what to look for. A man will work for money to buy food, clothing and a roof over his head with a warm place to sleep just to survive. A mountain man will hunt, fish for food, build his own shelter and when money is needed, he will trap, sell his pelts, pan for gold and mine for gemstones to sell for supplies he needs, he does all that to survive, but you have to love it, or it will not work for you. Surviving in the mountains is difficult for many, but just a way of life for others, they don't look at the difficult part."

Sloppy told Alan he had done well for his family and had proved he knew how to survive mountain life; he was doing good by teaching Yano survival skills that would come in handy as he got older.

"The next time we see you we will have another child for you to meet," said Alan.

Sloppy congratulated him and said he would stop by in a few months to meet the new family member, "you and Odina are great parents, and your children are lucky to have you just like y'all are blessed to have them."

As their conversation continued, Sloppy went on to tell Alan there were larger veins of gold in the region than anyone knew about. "You hear talk about not being enough gold here for prospectors to waste their time and that is why it must be a well-kept secret. I know more than I have told you and I believe you know more than you have told me. When we sell our gold, it is always best not to speak of the area it came from and that is the good thing about dealing with Beanstalk, he never asks, he just wants to buy, and turns it around quickly, he makes good money and never has to work for it like the gold miner does."

Alan could sit on the porch and talk with Sloppy all night, but he had to go to work the next morning, so he needed to turn in. They would have breakfast early with plenty of coffee.

Alan told Sloppy what a pleasure it was to have him visit. There were candles in the bunkhouse for light and a two eyed coal heater if he needed it to stay warm. Sloppy thanked them for being so kind to him and said if it was okay, he would ride into town with him in the morning after breakfast.

After breakfast, they saddled up and headed to town. When they passed the Bolins, Alan shared with Sloppy about Clyde being bedridden for a while, a four-hundred-pound hog ran into him and broke his right leg and left ankle, and he stopped by after work each day to help with the chores and check on him.

Sloppy knew Clyde and Tehya, "they are good people, and he was sorry to hear about their bad luck, Clyde had always been a hard worker, so laying up in bed couldn't be easy for him."

When they arrived in town, Sloppy said he would stay the night in town once he took care of business with Beanstalk, but he would stop by their place on his way back to the mountains.

Alan reminded him the bunkhouse was always open for him anytime he came through and he hoped to see him in a few months.

The workday was finished, and Alan stopped by the Bolins again. He could see Dr. Hogue was there and he hoped Clyde was doing better. Tehya met him all smiles, the Dr. was with Clyde, and he was doing much better, thanks to Dr. Hogue and you and Odina. He had been up several times during the day on crutches.

Alan was so happy to hear the good news and he told Tehya he wanted to check on the boys and see if they needed help with the chores.

She said they were caught up with everything and had gone to the river to fish.

Dr. Hogue had finished with Clyde and told Alan he wanted to stop by and check on Odina while he was down this way.

34. Better Change

Dr. Hogue and Alan arrived at the cabin to find Odina sitting on the porch making necklaces, she was glad to see Dr. Hogue, it would save her a trip into town tomorrow for a checkup. Yano was playing in front of the cabin when he saw his dad was home, he came running asking always if he could ride Smokie.

Alan told him not right now, go play and explore and tell me later what you found.

Dr. Hogue and Odina went inside, after several minutes they both came outside smiling at Alan.

He asked if everything was good to which Dr. Hogue said, "Yes, both babies sound healthy."

Alan's mouth dropped open, his eyes got larger, and he said, "You said both babies, are we having twins?"

"Yes, you are," said Doc, "there are two heart beats."

Odina was happy, but a little worried about taking care of two instead of one, but she knew they could and would do fine. They were both in shock at the news of twins but more excited than worried. Odina wanted them to be thinking of names for boys and girls,

Alan agreed, they should have a list of Cherokee names to honor their tribal heritage and a list of Scottish names to honor Scottish heritage, so they decided to write down a list of names and when it was closer to time for the babies to be born, they would pick two meaningful girl names and two for boys.

Alan called for Yano to come; they could ride for a little while before supper. He put a bridle on PoGo and Smokie and helped Yano up. Riding down Three Bears Trail toward the Bolins, they turned and rode off to the left, Alan wanted to look at the land that joined theirs on the south end, it would make very good pastures to raise cattle, he was always thinking ahead for ways to provide for his family. For now, the plans would be put on hold for the time being, he has more important things to do now. He told Yano to lead the way back home, so they could finish chores before supper. What he really wanted to do was to watch Yano and see how he handled Smokie. Smokie started to gallop, and Alan was amazed at how his small young son sat on his horse and rode so well. They arrived back at the barn, took care of the horses and Alan had Yano fed the chickens some scratch feed while he gathered stove wood and a couple buckets of water for use in the cabin.

Odina was cooking supper and still smiling, but a little bit in shock at the news of having twins.

They all went to the front porch after supper. "What did you see Yano while you were exploring today," Alan asked.

He said he found some pretty rocks, saw a lizard that was fast and then he went to the back, there he saw deer and rabbit tracks.

"That is good, I am proud of you, but why did you think the rocks were pretty."

Yano said because they were green, he guessed.

"Can you show me where you found the green rocks?"

"Yes Sir," and he pointed down the hill from the porch, so Alan asked him to walk him to the pretty rocks, he would like to see them. Yano led his father to the green rocks and there were several about the size of a pea laying on top of the ground.

When he saw them, he knew they were Jade or Emeralds and it looked like more could be found with a little more digging.

Alan picked up the rocks, put them in Yano's hand and told him to go show them to his mother.

Odina said, "There are treasures all over this land and they would put the rocks in a little wooden box and every time he found more, he could add them to the box."

Yano was happy his mother and father liked his pretty green rocks.

It was now the first of June 1853, and they were about one month away from having two more babies added to the Adams' family, they can't wait to meet the two additional treasures.

Alan had built another cradle frame for a double hammock and Odina had made two baskets out of wisteria vines shaped like eggs. Alan would attach each basket to the cradle frame to hold each baby so there would be no fear of them falling out. He also made Yano a rope swing and hung it from a large tree in front of the cabin.

Alan and Odina were both a year older now, his birthday was March 11th and Odina's was April 15th.

Their neighbor and friend, Clyde had gotten over the pneumonia a couple of months ago and the leg and ankle had healed to where he could walk again without crutches even though he walked with a limp.

Tehya and Nova make daily visits to help Odina with any chores that needed to be done and Tehya would be there for the birth of the twins just like she was when Yano was born.

Alan was able to kill a big boar bear last spring to help feed his family, he never wasted anything he killed, they learned to survive on what the land provided to them. They were able to purchase a mule to plow and pull heavy loads. Alan planted corn, potatoes and beans every year and was able to pay Ridge and Lucus to help with planting and cutting wood for cooking and heating.

Yano also joined Ridge and Lucas; they are good friends despite the age difference. There have been some bumps and bruises, mostly on Yano, but life is good at the Adams paradise.

The coal mining business was still going strong with no mining accidents since Alan had been appointed Safety Inspector, only a fire in one of the smaller shanties where two miners lived. No one was injured but the shanty was badly damaged, so the men moved in with other miners until they had time to rebuild.

35. Time is Near

Friday, July the second, Alan left for work as usual. Tehya came before he left which made him feel better about leaving Odina since the birth of the twins was so close.

When he got home from work, Dr. Hogue was there checking on her. He and Tehya both knew the babies were coming soon, so Tehya left to go home and prepare supper for her family, and she would come back in a couple hours and stay the night.

Dr. Hogue was glad since he had other people to check on and could not stay, but he would be back around eight tomorrow morning and planned on staying until they were born, he believed it would be around lunchtime. Tehya and Dr. Hogue both were very accurate on Yano's time of birth, so Alan was confident with their predictions.

He stayed up all night drinking coffee on the front porch leaving the front and back doors open for a little breeze to come through so he could hear if Odina was having contractions.

Odina was sleeping well, and Tehya was napping lightly as the sun came up over the mountain behind the cabin.

Alan nodded off on the front porch.

Odina woke up while Tehya was preparing breakfast, they found Alan asleep on the porch and decided to let him sleep, he had been up all night.

Dr. Hogue rode up around eight thirty and Alan woke when he heard the horse and buggy pull up to the front porch. He jumped up, ran inside to find Odina, Yano and Tehya at the table eating breakfast.

Odina immediately saw the scared look on his face, smiled and said, "Not yet, we didn't want to wake you, come and have breakfast."

Dr. Hogue walked in, "What about me," he said.

They all laughed and asked him to have breakfast and coffee, they did not hear him pull up.

Alan and Yano usually took care of the chores before breakfast, but today they would wait until afterwards. As soon as they finished eating, Alan told Yano to come with him to milk the cow, feed the chickens and gather eggs.

Odina began having contractions while they were handling the chores. As her contractions became closer together, Dr. Hogue told her it was time; the babies were arriving; the first one was born at 9:30 and the second one came fifteen minutes later at 9:45.

When Alan and Yano were at the chicken coop, he heard a baby crying. He told Yano to go to his swing and play until he called him back to the house. As he approached the front door, he heard a cry with a different tone than the first and he knew both babies had arrived.

Dr. Hogue said, Congratulations, you are now blessed with a beautiful little girl and a handsome little boy."

Alan was speechless.

Dr. Hogue said, "they are perfectly healthy, and Odina did very well and asked Alan to retrieve his scales from his buggy so he could document their weight." He wrote July 3, 1853, on his notepad, birth time for the baby girl was 9:30 and for the baby boy was 9:45, the baby girl weighted five pounds ten ounces and the baby boy was six pounds six ounces.

Tehya wrapped the babies in a blanket and laid them on Odina's chest.

Alan pulled up a chair next to her admiring his twins. He pulled the list of names out of his pocket, they listed two boy names and two girl names and agreed if they had a girl and a boy, they would take the first name listed for each, so their daughter was named Ayita Grace Adams. Ayita in Cherokee meant 'First to Dance'. Their son was named Koda James Adams. Koda in Cherokee meant 'Little Bear'. Alan gave the names to Dr. Hogue so he could complete the birth certificates. Alan went to the front porch and called for Yano to come and meet his little sister and brother.

Yano came running, so excited to see his sister and brother.

Dr. Hogue checked the babies and Odina once more before he left. He was pleased with the health of all three.

Alan told Dr. Hogue they seemed to be a bit small, and he said they were smaller than Yano, but there were two of them and together they weighed about four pounds more than Yano when he was born. He would be back Tuesday or Wednesday to check on Odina and the babies unless he was needed before then and he would bring the birth certificates with him. It sounded good to Alan; he told Dr. Hogue he would stop by his office on Monday to settle the bill for his services.

Tehya and Nova came every day for a few weeks to help Odina and Nova planned to come often to watch Yano and the twins so Odina could tend to her chores. They are forever grateful for friends like the Bolins.

The twins were very good babies and Yano would not leave their side for long, he's already planning on teaching them everything he has learned. Alan and Odina are feeling blessed.

36. Mountain Life History

Mountain living was a hard life, but it was a simple way of life for the Adams, they were taught at an early age how to survive by living off the land.

Being honest, hardworking, trustworthy, sharing, caring and secretive was how they lived their life and raised their children the same way.

The year was now 1860, Abraham Lincoln had been elected the sixteenth President of the United States. Alan and Odina had welcomed their fourth child, a daughter Nokomis Skye Adams on September 24, 1855.

The mining business had been operational for twelve years and was getting close to shutting down. There were plans to start a new mining operation sixty miles northeast of Shepherd Springs. Mr.

Stockburn talked with Alan about being his Superintendent over the new mine. Alan, only thirty years old, had worked for Mr. Stockburn for the twelve years it had been open, but he had over twenty years' experience in the mining business. He truly loved his job but was torn on whether to move his family to the new location, or possibly leave his family here on the land they loved. The decision would require a lot of thinking and talking with Odina on the front porch. There might be a few more months of work left before he must give Mr. Stockburn an answer.

In 1856, Alan and Odina purchased two hundred more acres that joined their south boundary line, giving them a total of one thousand acres of land. With the help of Yano, Ridge and Lucas, he had fenced in fifty acres and had twenty head of cattle that Yano and Koda helped with.

He had not heard from his old friend Sloppy in several months but that's not uncommon, sometimes he didn't see him for a year, but Sloppy was getting older and Alan was getting a little concerned. Sloppy had still not taken Alan to his place deep in the mountains and Alan had not been in the area Sloppy described as being the way to find his place, but he was confident he could find it. If he didn't hear from him soon, he would take a couple days to locate him and make sure everything was alright.

Every evening after supper, Alan would sit on the front porch thinking and listening to the magical sounds of the Appalachian Mountains. Tonight, he was weighing the pros and cons of the new coal mining job. The only pro he could think of would be better pay, but there were a lot of bad points also. He really loved the work and was good at it and thankful Mr. Stockburn had hired him twelve years ago just on the word of a fellow miner from High Point. He didn't want to disappoint him by turning down the offer, but hoped he would understand if that was his decision.

Odina joined him on the porch, and they watched the three youngest play in the dirt and swing on the rope. Yano had gone to the barn to check on the horses.

Alan asked Odina if she believed the Spirit of the Wolf lived sixty miles from Shepherd Springs at the new location.

Odina doesn't know if the Spirit of the Wolf lives there, but she knew it lives here and was their protector.

At this moment, all is right in their world.

The End